BARTON

STRONG MANOR Book 4

KATHI S. BARTON

This is a work of fiction. Names, characters, places, and incidents are products of the author's imagination or are used fictitiously and are not to be construed as real. Any resemblance to actual events, locations, organizations, or persons, living or dead, is entirely coincidental.

World Castle Publishing, LLC
Pensacola, Florida
Copyright © 2024 Kathi S. Barton
Paperback ISBN: 9798891261440
eBook ISBN: 9798891261457
First Edition World Castle Publishing, LLC, February 9, 2024
http://www.worldcastlepublishing.com
Licensing Notes
Cover: Karen Fuller
Editor: Karen Fuller

Chapter 1

Walking toward the hotel room he'd been staying in after work, Barton slowed his steps to pause and listen. No music. By the time he was halfway to his room over the last few weeks, he could not only hear music blasting, but it would be vibrating along the walls, too. He did wonder how the other people in the hotel could stand it, either. Putting his card into the door lock, he closed his eyes and entered the room, careful of where he stepped as usual. Leaning back against the door, he relished the quiet, even if it was only for a few minutes.

Tessa Brown, niece to John Chase, had been living with him for the past several weeks while the two of them cleaned up the mess that had been at a recent factory that he'd been sent to check on. It just so happened that while Barton was there trying to figure out why the company that had been in business for several generations was losing money handing food, Tessa had been sent as well to check on things. She was a state inspector for food industries and was working for someone who had called off sick that morning.

The little cake factory had been built on land that his family owned, and had asked for their help with an expansion that they were considering. Tessa had shown up as the state's health inspector, and the two of them, with the help of the police, had had the place shut down when they'd found not just rats in the place but also dirty practices — barefooted workers, smoking and a plethora of other things going on while they were cooking that made him so ill that morning that he still couldn't eat any sweets without getting slightly sick.

Barton might not have met Tessa previously if not for the fact that John, her uncle, had been trying to sell off the land that had been left to his sister when her husband had passed away — completely unrelated to the factory but just a coincidence really that the two of them had hooked up. Barton was happy for the time with her — at first. However, he was thrilled beyond words that he'd seen a part of her that—Christ, he thought. She was the biggest slob he'd ever encountered. It wasn't just her being a slob that had pissed him off, but that she didn't understand why it had upset him so much that she'd never picked up anything. Not even a toilet paper roll or used tissues that she tossed at the trash can and never hit. It, along with her eating in bed habits that had driven him to the brink of asking her to leave.

Making his way to the bedroom of the suite that he was using, he nearly sat on the edge of the bed to call to the front desk. It was such a mess, not just the room but the entire suite, that he wanted to either leave it and take another room or have someone come and clean it. Again. When the man at the front desk answered, he had to take a deep breath before talking to him.

"This is Barton Strong. I was wondering if you have someone on staff who could come and clean my room for me. I know that it's been done already, but it could...I won't lie to you. It's a mess here, and I'll pay whatever it takes to have it stripped down and recleaned. Sheets, towels, everything cleaned." The man said he'd have a crew up there in a moment. "Thank you so much. Please let them know that I'm sorry for this mess and that…I'll make it worth their while to do this for me."

"Very good, sir. I'm sending up three to…I believe this crew has cleaned your room before, sir." It hurt him that he'd been, through no fault of his own, having extra help to clean his place without complaint. "Before I forget to tell you again, sir, when Ms. Brown left today, she turned in her pass key."

Barton wanted to tell the man that she'd not be back with him ever again but he was sure that anyone on the floor he was on heard them arguing last night. It had been an ongoing event for the last two nights, the two of them coming to a head about not just the room—though that was bad enough but their lack of compatibility on a great many levels, as it turned out. Last night, it had all come to a head when all he'd wanted her to do was to clean up after herself. And to—a big one to him, stop fucking eating in the bed.

"Thank you so much for that information. I will make sure that I take care of the help when I'm ready to leave the day after tomorrow. You can count on it." He would too. Leave the three of them a hefty tip even if he had to go to the bank to get cash for them. "I'll wait for them to come up, then get out of their way by going to the dining room for dinner. I'll be there if they have any questions. Or concerns, for that matter."

After the three women showed up, he got their names so that when he did leave, he would know who to leave the tips to. Giving them each two hundred dollars for them helping him now, he hoped that they'd be kind enough to make sure he didn't come back to anything that resembled the room he had now.

The dining room in the hotel was top-notch. He loved their simple menu and the great chef who was behind the food. Tonight, he was going to have what he wanted and how he wanted it cooked. That had been another argument that he'd had with Tessa. She was forever changing his order on every little thing that he did. He should have seen her for what she was the first night they'd had dinner, but he had been getting laid regularly, and that had fogged up his head. He'd learned a valuable lesson in that.

"You don't need to have your steak rare, Bart," she would say to him. Not only would she have him order a chicken breast, but she would call him that ridiculous shortened version of his first name. "I don't like to see blood all over your plate. It makes me ill. You don't want me to be ill, do you?" It wasn't until the end of their stay together that he realized that her voice would go all whiney-like. Christ, that would have been the first thing his family would have noticed.

So he relented. Several times over the course of the few weeks they'd been together, he'd not get what he wanted anywhere if she was with him. Tonight, he was going to have not just a steak, which he loved, rare Pittsburgh style, but he was going to have mushrooms on the side along with a baked potato with the works—French fries were *not* the only thing to go with steak according to Tessa—as well as French onion soup and bread sticks. He was going to eat every bite of it, even if he was going to be slightly uncomfortable when he was finished. Smiling to himself, he also ordered himself a beer, something that she told him she hated the smell of. This was his dinner, damn it.

When his cell phone rang, he nearly didn't answer it. But when he saw his brother's goofy face as he pulled it the rest of the way out of his pocket, he was glad to hear from him. Maverick was a nerd about numbers, but he was a lot funnier than the rest of his family. He started out by telling him how he'd heard from Trevor, who was on another site like he was for a company issue.

"You think things will be sorted out soon there? I know that you're going to have the building torn down. Christ, I read the report about the factory, and it turned me off of sweets forever, I think." Barton told him that he hadn't had any since he'd been there the first day. "Did you read the report? It said that there was such an infestation of rats in that place that as soon as the heavy loaders hit the wall, they had to run from their dozers because the rats there had swarmed them. Christ, I can't imagine what—"

"Enough. Please." He was glad that he'd finished eating before talking to his brother. "Something less nasty, please. Has Jade's mom had the baby yet?"

Jade, Jenson's wife, was going to adopt her mother's baby when he was born. Hilda felt that she was too old to raise a baby properly and had asked if Jade would do it. It was going to work out well for all parties as Jenson was excited to become a dad so soon after marrying Jade, and they were planning more kids. Jenson was also working to become the congressman to their state and on to being president when he had enough work under his belt to do that.

He was extremely proud of his brother and sister-in-law.

"Not yet. It's driving her crazy to be on bed rest, though. Being in her forties and having such a large baby was really taking its toll on her. Jade said that she's enjoying having her mom around to talk to, but she knew that she'd not be able to just lay around like her mother is." Barton said he didn't think he could do it either. He liked to be moving. "So, have you gotten Tessa squared away?"

Trevor was the only one who knew how much trouble he was having with Tessa. He'd called him the first time she'd begged him to have unprotected sex with her. He didn't do that. None of his unmarried brothers would have unprotected sex with any woman that they were seeing. But the morning he'd woke up with her on his naked cock had been the final straw. That had been two mornings ago and the last time he'd slept with her. Christ, he'd been terrified and was still a little that she might have gotten what she wanted. Even though she had said she just wanted natural sex and didn't want a child either, he no more believed her than Trevor did when he told him about it. It had been one argument after another with her since that morning.

"She moved out today. After making a mess — it's really not that she made a bigger mess than she normally does, but I couldn't take it anymore. Who tears all the blankets off the bed and tosses them to the floor to have a meal in the bed? No one but her. Then there are the towels. Why did it take her five towels to dry? Sure, she wrapped her hair in one of them, but what about the other four? She's gone, and I couldn't be happier. And if you ask me, this is the perfect reason for me not to have a wife. I'm too picky about how they leave things." Trevor asked him if he tossed out his personal things. "You mean my toothbrush? Yes. I tossed out not only that but the paste, my hair brush, and anything that I used to clean up with. I picked myself up replacements on my way here tonight. Hoping and counting that she was gone. I'm so very glad that she is, Trevor. I don't know how much longer — did I tell you that I didn't invite her to stay here in the first place? She just showed up with her things on the first day." Barton let himself into his room after being told that it was ready and smiled at the cleanliness of his room. The smell was wonderful as well.

"You told me." Barton leaned back in his chair as he looked around his room. "Are you in your room now? I have some things that I want you to look at on your computer."

"Yes, hang on." The two of them went over contracts for the next hour. When he stepped into the bathroom to change into something more comfy, he touched all the clean towels there and even set out his toothbrush and hairbrush. It was his space, and he was never so happy to not have to share as he was right then. Barton didn't want to share his things ever again. He was going to stay single from now on just so he'd not have to do that. Women were messy, and he wasn't in the mood, he thought, to be made to be messy, too.

After getting off the computer and phone with his brother, Barton undressed and got into bed. The sheets were soft and tight on the mattress. All the pillows were there for him to use, and when he turned off the light, he was equally thrilled that there wasn't a glow from someone else's phone or the television blaring some music well into the morning.

He did feel slightly bad for the argument that they'd had. Barton had been careful not to say things that he would regret later. Also, he didn't call her names, though she didn't have any trouble with calling him all kinds of names. Now that he thought about it, being away from her, he could see that he had really wanted it to work, to have someone in his life as a stable person, but he'd rushed things, or they both had, and he was glad that he'd made his mistake on his own rather than getting her moved into his home where his family might well have been hurt when their relationship had gone to shit.

~*~

Toria didn't say anything while the argument went on around her. There were a lot of different subjects that she could have commented on, but she kept her opinions to herself. Not that it would have done her any good to have spoken, but she was able to observe her family at their not-so-best.

When Jake, the house butler, entered the room, she smiled at him when he looked in her direction. Putting out her hand, she received not just a cup of tea, which she desperately needed, but a warm cinnamon bun, too. Thanking him, she watched as he maneuvered around the furniture and people to lay out the rest of the treats he'd brought in. Toria looked at her dad when he looked at her.

"Well? Do you have anything to add to this? I'm not saying that it will do any good, but I'd like to have your—"

"Of course, she has an opinion of what is going on. She forever has to put her two cents in where it's none of her concern." Toria said nothing to her sister, who had called them all here in the first place. "Well? What is it, Victoria? Tell me how you would have done things differently so that you weren't left at the altar."

"Lorie, don't be so dramatic. You weren't left at the altar. You weren't even picking out wedding invitations with him." Her mother looked at her as she continued. "Do hand me one of those napkins, Toria. And if you can reach it, would you be so kind as to pour me some tea?"

Jake poured tea for not just her mom but her father, too. Toria didn't engage with her sister while she finished her bun. First of all, she knew that whatever she said wouldn't be welcomed, and secondly, she wanted to eat her breakfast, no matter how small it was, so that she could get out of there faster. When she finished, licking her fingers for effect, Toria grinned at her grannie when she laughed.

"Why does everyone take her advice over mine?" Grannie pointed out to Lorie that Toria hadn't said a word yet, but Lorie wasn't having it. "It's not as if she wasn't left standing there too."

That statement might have hurt her years ago, but she had been widowed seven years ago, not left at the altar. Not to mention, she and Sherman had been married for a full year before he had died. Picking up another bun that she wasn't sure that she wanted, Toria looked at her sister.

"I don't know why you're surprised that Jimmy left you, Lorie. The two of you fought more than you were friendly together. Not to mention, you told us when you first started dating each other that he didn't want to marry. Not ever. So why you're suddenly surprised that he told you he wasn't going to propose to you is beyond anyone sitting in this room." Lorie claimed that she loved him. "No, you didn't. You loved what he might represent to you in the way of a rich husband. The two of you bickered more like you and I do every time you were together more than you did as a loving couple."

"I suppose you never fought with Sherman. That he was the perfect man for you. Well, I don't want a perfect man." Toria snorted and told her that she was far from perfect herself. "You bitch."

"Mommy?" Before she could put her teacup aside, she was holding her son, Shermie. Perfect timing, she thought before she and Lorie got into another fight that would have her parents upset. "I was outside with Grannie's dog, and he pooped in the yard. Wanna come and see it?"

"Thanks, but I'll pass." He was six and liked six-year-old stuff. He could and would defuse an argument between her and Lorie faster than her dad could. Dad took her son to the kitchen, holding onto his humor as he told him that they'd wash up. Toria looked at Lorie. "When are you going to get it through your thick head that no one is going to marry you because you want them to. You can't order someone to love you. You can't even make someone like you. Just fucking grow up." Mom told her to watch her language. Growling low in her throat, she told her mom that she was sorry, then added that it was true.

"True or not, you don't have to use that language around here, honey. What if your son started using that word?" She didn't tell her that he had done that already, but Mom looked at Lorie. "Just as your sister said, he told you that he wasn't going to marry you. He only wanted to hang out with you a little before he made his way back to college. You yourself told me that he wasn't the type of person that you wanted in a husband. I don't have any idea why you think that just because he left—as he said he was going to do—to go back to school, you took that to mean that he left you like he was going to marry you at any second. Lorie, you're only eighteen years old. Far too young to be trying to make someone marry you. If this is finished here, and I'm telling you that it is, I have two meetings that I have to attend, not to mention that Shermie and I are having dinner together. It's our date night."

"Why are you going out to dinner with a six-year-old when I'm right here?" Lorie went after Mom, telling her that she should be taking her out to dinner and not a kid. Toria looked at her grannie when she laughed.

"I'd like to tell your mother to take Lorie out so that she can teach her some manners at the dinner dates, but I doubt that it would end well for either of them. Besides, I think that Hanna enjoys having Shermie as her date more than she does my son. How is he doing now that you have him in private school, Toria?" She told her grannie that he was adjusting better than he had been before. "I would never have thought that he could do well at public school with the way his upbringing has been. How many times have the two of you circled the globe? Seven? Eight? Why the boy knows more languages than I do and

I'm older. He's a smart little man, too, isn't he?"

"Yes. Right now, he's taking high school classes along with a few college ones to keep him happy. And I love the fact that he can come here with mom and dad and be a kid. I believe that was the problem with his stressing out when he was in public school. There was never any time set aside for him to be a six-year-old." Grannie told her that he was very good at being a six-year-old. "I agree. And I don't want him to ever forget that."

"You won't allow him to be anything but happy. He couldn't have been born to a better mother than you, Toria." She thanked her grannie. "What are you going to do about Lorie? She's going to be driving everyone crazy until she finds herself some other man to cling to. I've never seen a child so hyped up to be married than she is. I think she's been talking about it since she was ten years old."

"I was eighteen when I got married." Grannie told her that she and Sherman had been together for a very long time. "Yes, since I was in kindergarten and he was in first grade. Once I saved him from a dog on the playground, then we never separated. However, I don't know that things would have lasted between us. Not if we were getting married today. Things are so much different nowadays."

"I'm glad that you see it that way, child. I want you to be happy again. I don't think that you've been happy or dating, for that matter, for a long time, have you?" She shrugged; this was a conversation that she would only have with her grannie. They were closer than she and her mom were. "I know that there is someone out there for you. For Lorie, too, if she were to ever give herself time to grow up. But you'll see. Someone will come along and sweep you off your feet, and you'll be as happy as you ever had been."

"That would be nice, but I'm not a single person. They'd have to love my son, too. And we both know that he has his own difficulties when it comes to trusting people." They both nodded. Shermie was terrified of men thanks to him being kidnapped when he'd been four. He only trusted people that were in his family and no one else. She glanced at the clock over the fireplace. "I have to get going. I have several meetings today before you and I have the one at the bank. Are you ready for it?"

"I am. I'm bringing our attorney, too. Things should be cut and dry, however, you never know about people and money." Toria said she knew that. After hugging and kissing Shermie and her parents, she left the house with Grannie. "Since mom is having dinner with Shermie, your father and I are having dinner. Why don't you join the two of us? It might be fun for us. You know that your dad can be counted on for a good laugh or two."

"I have so much—Never mind. I'll join you. I was going to say I have a lot of work to get done, but I was informed this morning by my son that I work too hard and need to take a break, too." Grannie said she was going to hug that kid. "Yes, I will as well. I'll be there. We can go over to the restaurant after the bank. All right?"

"Great." With a kiss on her cheek, she left her grannie and got into her car. Grannie worked harder than any other person she knew half her age, and she loved her to pieces. As Toria made her way to the office, she called to make sure that her schedule was just as tight as it had been when she'd been summoned home by her sister.

"Mr. Barkley Strong is running behind, so I moved the meeting around that you had with Mr. Beatty. Both men are all right with the change. Mr. Strong said that he was bringing his son with him as he had a better handle on the terms of the agreement than he did." Toria asked if he'd gone over the contract. "He has. I don't think Mr. Beatty is going to be all that happy with the changes to it. I'm assuming that you've gotten the changes as well? I sent them out to you last night."

"I read them over this morning. No, you're right. He's not going to be happy with the changes. But he's lucky that they're even considering loaning him more money when he's only paid back about half of the other loan that we've set up for him. Mr. Strong was wonderful in making sure that our fees were paid off first." Becky told her that she had the same layout for drinks as she had before. "Good. I know that Mr. Strong won't partake, but Beatty acts like he's never had a meal before. I'm pulling into the lot now. I'll be up in a few moments."

Toria was a lending broker for large companies wanting to expand and or renew their equipment. She'd used the Strong Foundation several times over the course of her job and enjoyed working with them. She'd only been working with Barkley and his wife Lisa so far, but she'd heard great things about his sons. This would be her first encounter with one of his children, and she thought that he was grooming them to take over his job. Mr. Strong, she knew, was a great man. She only hoped that his children were as well in the world of business.

By the time Beatty showed up, she had made a lot of notes on the contract between his business and the Strong Foundation. There were several places that she was going to make sure that Beatty understood that had to be adhered to, but she was mostly worried about the timeline that had been set up on the payment plan. Mr. Strong, Barkley, as he asked her to call him showed up at the same time.

"If you're ready, Ms. Davies, we can get this started. Hopefully, Mr. Beatty is ready as we are." She said that she'd not had a chance to talk to him yet but would ask. "He's called my office several times over the last two days trying to negotiate better terms, he called them. I don't do business that way. I believe he was trying to cut you out of the deal we have."

"Really? Well, that explains a great deal. He asked if he could have a long conversation with you without me in the room. I don't work that way either. Thank you for giving me a heads up." Barkley told her it was his pleasure. Then he introduced her to his son. "It's good to meet you, Jenson. I've heard good things about you and your political stands. You have my vote."

"Thank you. I appreciate all the votes I can get." They entered the conference room just as Beatty was stuffing his face with pastries. From the look of his tie, he'd not bothered with any sort of napkins that were there with the food. There was so much filling on it that it looked like he was working on an art project using food. "Mr. Beatty, my name is Jenson Strong. I'm here with my father to help expedite this transaction."

"Yes, well, I want to talk to your father alone, if you don't mind." Jenson sat down and said that he did mind. "Well, I don't believe that we can do business then. As I said to your father several times, I'm not at all happy with my representation with this firm."

Jenson and Barkley both stood up. Joining them moving toward the door, she heard Beatty stand up and they were out the door before he started yelling at them to return or he was going to leave too. Not that it mattered to her one way or the other at this point. Toria had already decided that she wasn't going to do anything for the Beatty Furniture's ever again.

"I wanted to talk to you, too, Toria. I do believe that your company and ours can do some very good work together from now on." Toria asked him what he had in mind. "Very good. I expected, though I have no idea why I would after working with you as long as I have, that you'd just turn me down. I would like for us to become one company. I'm not going to suggest that I buy you out. Frankly, I don't think that we'd do much good being one company like that. However, I would like to invest in your company, say fifty-fifty, on everything that you do. I believe, and my dad will agree with me, that as two companies under one roof, we can do more work than having you simply come to us when you have a big hitter that needs money."

"All right. But you do know that I work with partners. My family, of course, but I would have to talk to them about it before I can make any decision. My grannie, Victoria Dutch, I believe you know her, and my dad, Warren Dutch, are my partners and would have to have a say in what I can do." Jenson told her that he didn't expect anything less from her. "Thank you for that. I will tell you this, my father has been thinking of retiring to be able to spend more time with my mom. They're planning a cruise for next month, and I think he wants to be able to not have to worry about anything while he's gone."

"You have a son." She asked him what that had to do with anything. "Nothing. I didn't mean to imply it did. I saw the pictures on your credenza behind you, and it occurred to me. I'm sorry if I offended you."

"I do have a son. Yes. My parents want to spend more time with him as well." Jenson nodded as he stretched out his legs. "I know your wife, Jade. She and I went to grade school together with my late husband, Sherman Davies."

"I'll ask her about it." Jenson laughed a little. "My mother-in-law is set to have a baby soon, and my wife and I are going to adopt him as our own. Maybe you can give us some pointers on raising a son."

"It's doubtful that your wife will need any advice. I remember her having all her ducks in a row every day. But I would like to help if you think that I can." They both agreed to meet up for dinner soon, and Jenson invited her for dinner. "I can't tonight. I'm having—you should join us. I'm having dinner with my dad and grannie tonight. This might be the perfect time to talk over business with you. I know that my grannie would love to talk to you about it. Dad? Well, he'll be sulking because he didn't get to have dinner with my mom and son. Mom is teaching Shermie how to behave like a gentleman while having dinner in public. You know, the usual things like how to order, be polite to the servers. I'm impressed with him each time they come home."

"My dad did the same to us when we were younger. Not as young as six, mind you, but we did get a head start on other young men that we grew up with." Jenson smiled at her. "I can imagine if he's in high school, as I've read, he must get teased a great deal."

Toria didn't say anything to his observation. Her son did get teased but it was the bullying that bothered them both a great deal.

Once it was set up with her family, they were going to meet at the restaurant together. She was nearly out of the building when Beatty met her at the door. He was spitting mad for being abandoned, but she had security escort him out, and that was good for both parties. They weren't going to help Beatty either, as it turned out.

Chapter 2

Barton was ever so glad to be home. While he'd been waiting for the crew to show up at the factory to take it to the ground, he'd started looking for homes on a website closer to his home. Living in the hotel for the past few months with different jobs made him realize how much he wanted his own space. A yard with a pool was one of the main things that he was looking for. But not having people he didn't know going in and out of his room was something that he didn't like all that much. Of course, he'd have help around the house, but he would know them, and it wasn't the same, he kept telling himself with a grin.

He had four houses that he liked so far that he'd found. One of them, the smaller of the four, had a pool, but it looked to him like it was small from the pictures. If the patio furniture was any indication of how big it was — or, in this case, small, he wasn't going to enjoy it. He was a tall man and wanted to be able to do laps without having to turn every few feet. Smiling to himself as he decided that he needed to call a realtor in the morning, his cell phone rang, and he was happy to see that it was Jenson.

"Please tell me that you're home now." He said he'd just gotten there an hour ago. "Thank goodness. Dad and I were having dinner with some hopeful business partners, and Hilda is in labor. I want to be there with Jade and her. Dad said that he'd go to the meeting, even though I think that he'd rather be with us, but this is too important of a meeting to let slide. And I want to be there to see my son with Jade."

"Well, of course you do. What do you need for me to do? Anything, you know that." He told him where he had been headed and that Dad would need someone there that could answer legal questions. "I can do that. And I've not eaten yet, so this will work out."

"Christ, you have no idea how happy you've made me." After getting the details while he changed into something less comfy, he was out the door and his phone on speaker phone just as his brother was waiting to head to the hospital. "I'll let you guys know when I know anything about our son. That sounds so great—I love that I'm going to have a son. Either one will be just fine with me, but a son. I can't stop saying that I'm going to be a dad, either. Thanks again, Barton."

He was pulling into the parking lot of the restaurant when the family limo parked to let out his dad. After it dropped him off, taking Jenson to the hospital, he hugged his dad, and they went inside to be seated at their table. The other people they were meeting were running behind, so he read over the information while awaiting them. It really wasn't that much to read. Dad told him they were still in the *'working it out'* phase of this merger.

Victoria Dutch showed up first. He liked her immediately. Then, when her son, Warren Dutch, showed up, he and his dad were having a great time. Warren was telling them about his wife and grandson when his daughter showed up. Standing to shake hands with the woman, he was surprised when she handed him her cell phone.

"It's my mom. She is on her way here with my son, and she wants to make sure that you're all right with that. He's only six, but he's well-behaved. They were having dinner together, but something at the restaurant happened, and they thought it would be better if they left there to be around more people. I don't know. Just tell her if you think it will be all right if they join us or not." He put the phone to his ear and heard someone shouting. Barton asked her who the man was that was shouting. "That would be Mr. Beatty. He's pissed off because we're not doing business with him anymore. I've tried to tell him that I was there at the meeting this morning, so I know that he said he wasn't going to do business with us any longer. Your family said no, then we're not going to do business with him. End of subject. However, not for him, I guess." Before he could ask if they needed help, Hanna Dutch spoke.

"Hello? Young man, I can't hear you over this idiot here. The man is scaring my grandson to death." Barton asked her if she needed the police. "They're here. But Shermie is terrified of all the noise that this fool is making. We're not far from where you are. Is it all right if we join you?"

"Yes, of course." When he heard a scream, he asked what was going on. "We're outside of the restaurant, and Shermie is having a meltdown. We'll go on home. Tell—"

"I'm coming out there." After handing the

phone back to the younger woman, he told her briefly what was going on. When she followed him out of the place, telling his family that they'd be back, he was happy for the help. The little man was terrified, and Barton, trying his best to make a terrible situation better, reached down, picked the kid up, and held him to his shoulder. "I've got you. I promise you that he's not going to hurt you. You just hang on to me, and I won't allow him to harm you in any way. I swear to you that you're going to be all right." The little boy had tears running down his cheeks when he looked at him.

"He was screaming at us. It hurt my ears. Then he tried to take me from my grannie." When he laid his head on his shoulder, crying, Barton patted him on the back while addressing who he assumed was Mr. Beatty.

"What the hell are you going on about? Is this your normal way of doing business? By scaring children to the point of tears?" He said that he wanted to do business with Barkley Strong. "That's my father. If this is how you conduct business by threatening little boys and women, I'm going to tell him that you do not deserve anyone bailing you out. I'm assuming that's what you want."

"Your family might be rich, but I can assure you that I'm going to bring you down a few notches before I'm finished with you." Barton asked Mrs. Dutch and the other woman to go inside and that he'd wait for the police. "You can't have me arrested. I'm only trying to keep my company afloat. You have no right to treat me like this. You do know that it's going to reflect badly on our future business dealings together. However, I'm not one to hold grudges, and I'm—"

"I have every right, you big blowhard." He turned to the woman, who still had no idea what her name was, and asked her if she was going to press charges. When she continued to stare at him with her mouth hanging open, it took him a few more times asking her before she spoke.

"He's never done that before." Barton told her that he was sure since he thought that he could get away with it that he had. "No. I mean, Shermie. He's never let anyone, men to be exact, to hold him before but my dad."

"He's scared." She nodded and asked what he'd said to her. "Do you want to press charges too? Your grandmother said that she was. The police are on their way. I would if I were you so that he'll be arrested. This is no way to conduct business, like he said, though I don't think he meant the same thing as we do."

When the police arrived, Beatty resisted arrest, trying to run away when he said that he was pressing charges and was charged with that as well. Handing off the little boy to his grandma so that she could take him inside, the boy held onto his hand and said that he wanted to stay. Barton didn't mind. It kept him from cursing, which is what he was nearly ready to do when Beatty tried to hit the woman. Barton turned to her when the officer asked him who was involved.

"Toria. My name is Toria Davies. This is my son, Shermie. And yes, I want to press charges. He threatened my grandmother, Victoria Dutch, and myself when he got here." The officer told her that she could come down to the station with the Strongs when she had time. "I'll do that. Thank you."

The two of them were left standing there with Shermie between them when the officer pulled out with Beatty in the back seat. After a few minutes of silence, he picked up Shermie again and asked her if she was going to join them. Nodding her acceptance, they entered the place together. He didn't know what was on the menu for a kid but figured that he'd eat something. Sitting him in a chair, Barton pulled out the chair for Toria and then sat himself.

Barton was surprised that no one spoke about Beatty. Usually, they didn't conduct business during meals, but this one was an exception as it had been set up as a business meeting. He was waiting on the kid to have a fit, or something he'd seen other kids do when out in a nice place like this one was. However, he smiled at him and put his hands in his lap, and only sniffled a little bit before being handed a tissue. He seemed all right after that.

Shermie didn't ask to play with anyone's cell phone to entertain himself, nor did he whine as he was sure other kids his age would have. He sat quietly and spoke when he was spoken to. He also ordered for himself, which Barton was very impressed with. Even ordering a steak for himself, he knew how he wanted it cooked, as well as asking for a side of mushrooms, just as he did with his own meal. While his family talked business, he was only there to answer legal questions that they might have. He talked to Shermie.

"You usually get a steak when you go out?" Shermie told him that it was his lesson in how to order it this time. He'd never had one before. "You'll enjoy it, I believe. You did a good job in ordering, too. But you know that cutting a steak can be tricky if you've never done it before. If I were you, I'd watch my dad do it. He's the one that taught us boys so that we'd not wear juice when we cut it up."

"Do you cut it all up in pieces before eating any of it? Grannie doesn't eat steak, but she said that she does that when she's having chicken. What do I do?" The whispered question didn't go unnoticed by his dad, who was sitting on the other side of him. Dad told him that you should cut it as you ate it. "Good. Thanks. Grannie thought that was what you did, but she wasn't sure. Thank you, Mr. Strong."

When his salad was brought to him, he was offered a booster chair. It was Dad who suggested that he sit in one. It wasn't because he was too short, but it was easier to cut steak when you could see down on it. Shermie sat in the chair brought to him, which did raise him up enough to look down at his plate and he seemed to be all right with it.

As the dinner progressed, Barton was impressed more and more with the Davies family. Toria had a good head on her shoulders about business and some of the things she thought that this merger was going to benefit her with, but Shermie also asked questions that he thought were well thought out. Like, would his mom be home nightly, and did she have to work all weekends.

"We all stop working at five. Unless something comes up at the last minute. While I would like to tell you that it's a done deal for you to do the same, Toria, I'm not going to assume anything for you. And we don't work on weekends. Unless, as I said, it's last minute. But we try very hard to not allow either one of those things to catch us off guard." Dad looked at him. "Barton here has been gone a month working on some problems that we had, and I know for a fact that he was getting off at a good time, around six, and didn't work on the weekends. Even though it could have brought him home earlier if he had, there has to be a work and health balance, or you're burnt out too soon. It's what happened to my father." Nodding, Barton continued on what his dad was saying.

"I got to do a bit of sightseeing while I was there. It was a lovely town, and I found some places that I thought that my parents would enjoy going to. We're all auction people, and a couple of auction houses made it on my list for them to go visit." Shermie asked him what an auction was. "It's where people have an auctioneer, sort of like a salesperson, come in and try to get the highest prices for things that they want to get rid of. Like household things. Antiques also, old coins and cars too. I'll take you to one sometime if you're ever around."

"I'd like that if mom says it's all right. I'm trying to expand my knowledge about all kinds of things." He nearly laughed but was glad that he didn't when he realized that Shermie was sincere about what he was saying. "I'd also like to go sightseeing with you, Mr. Strong. I love antique shops. Mom and I have fun looking up what the items in the store were used for. There are some strange things out there that we don't use anymore."

"My grandma has some odd items in her house, too. She has a rotary phone too that I used to play with when I would go visit her." Shermie told him that he'd seen one in a museum one time. "I bet. There is a nice museum near here too that you might like to go and see. It's one I've been to a lot and find something interesting every time I go."

After dinner was over and they had all declined desserts, it was time for them to part company. Barton would tell anyone who was around that he had had the best meal he'd ever had with a six-year-old at his side. His mom, too, was fun, but he wasn't on the lookout for a date, so he mostly ignored her for talking with her son. As soon as they were in the car to go home, his dad questioned him about Toria.

"I'd say she's a good mom. Which you've told me a million times, in doing business, you look at how a person treats others before making a decision. It couldn't have been easy for her to raise him after just losing her husband to cancer. And I love her grandmother. She's smart too and has a great head on her shoulders for all kinds of things." Dad told him that he had thought the same thing. "I am worried, however, about her work-to-home balance. Shermie told me that she gets home after he's gone to bed most nights. Do you think this will add more work to her or help her out? I'd hate to contribute to her overworking."

"Her father is retiring soon, too, he told me. I don't think that will make her any less of a work acholic than she is now." Dad asked him what he'd do. And he asked him what he meant. "Would you go into business with her if you knew that she's going to work herself into an early grave if she doesn't slow down? I would hate for anything to happen to her. Anyone for that matter, but like you, I do think she'll stress herself out more than she'll need to."

"Talk to her parents. They both seem to have a good relationship with her. Let them know, even if she's there, that you're concerned about her working too hard. For sure she needs a better secretary. Did you notice how many times she called her while we were eating? That shit wouldn't fly for any of us with her not making a decision at all without Toria okaying it. She's not been trained well, which I'm thinking might be it. Or she's been told to ask about everything going on. I'm thinking that would drive me crazy the first time she did it." Dad asked him about Tessa. "I don't want to talk about her. She's out of my life, and I'm glad that things progressed the way that they had before we started something serious."

"All right. But if you ever want to talk about it, just come over. I know that you had a blowout on that last night. Trevor told me that he'd heard from a friend of his who was staying at the same hotel." He told him that he was sorry for that. "Don't be. I know you well enough, son, that you'd not start something like that. All right. I'll set up a meeting with her family for soon and we'll go from there. Is the factory finished up?"

"Yes. We've been cautioned about building

there again. For at least a few years. We don't want to have an infestation even before the first wall goes up on something else." Dad agreed with him and shivered, too. "Christ, Dad, I don't know that I'll ever get that out of my head. It was the worst…never mind. It was just bad, and let's leave it at that."

Barton ended up staying at his parents' house that night. He enjoyed it, hanging out with his mom and dad and having them all to himself. As he was headed up to his old room, he could see where Clay and Lizzy were making progress on making the manor their home. Jenson was building a home instead of taking over the family home because of his political ambitions. Barton was proud of all his family but especially for Jenson as he was thinking of being president someday.

After taking a shower and pulling on something soft to wear to bed, Barton was in bed by ten. Something that he never did was go to bed before midnight, and he found that being home alone was just what he needed to get a very restful good night's sleep. Closing his eyes after pulling the blanket up and over him, Barton was as relaxed as he'd been in some time.

~*~

Shermie didn't tell anyone that he was being bullied at school. He figured that his mom had enough things to worry about on her plate, and she didn't need to know that he wasn't happy with the school that he was in. This was his third school in as many months. Walking to his locker to get his books for the rest of the day, Shermie felt someone punch the back of his head, then the front. Too fast for him to know what had happened.

When he opened his eyes, it terrified him for a few minutes as he couldn't see. Pulling the ice pack, what he found when he touched the cloth, the school nurse was standing over him. The big man had him cringing away from him.

"You've hit your head, Sherman. Would you please tell me what happened? I heard that you were trying to hide in your locker. What would you have done had you gotten in there and couldn't have gotten out? You might well have been there all week." Shermie just stared at the man, wondering why he'd think that he would even fit in the slim locker. "Well? Do you have anything to say about that?"

"I want my mom." The nurse, Mr. Coldwell, said he'd been trying to reach her. "Then my grandparents. Did you try them?"

"Yes. The number that I have has been changed, and they won't give the new one to me. I'm not finished talking to you about why you were trying to get into your locker." He said that he'd not, that he'd been hit from behind. "No one saw that. And we don't take kindly here in high school for kids to lie about things. Understand me?"

By the tone of his voice, Shermie knew that not only did Mr. Coldwell know what happened, but he also knew who had done it. Sitting up, he was nearly sick with the pain. And blood, warmer than the ice pack had been, was running down his face. Holding the rag there, he asked if he could call his friend. Someone who knows his family.

"Who? If you tell me that it's some kid, then I'm going to assume that you've made this arrangement today to get out of class. Is that what you've done, Sherman?" He said that he loved school and wouldn't want to miss anything about it. "Of course you do. You can call your friend, but I'm not going to let you go with just anyone."

Being handed the phone, he wondered about the paperwork that his mom had filled out before he was coming here. It had a list of the only people who could pick him up, even in an emergency. Calling

Mr. Strong, he was in tears by the time he got him on the phone.

"Mr. Strong, it's Sherman Davies." He knew it was the wrong Mr. Strong as soon as he asked him if he needed something. "You're Barton, aren't you? I was looking for your dad because the school nurse isn't going to let me go home with a kid."

"I don't believe anyone would mistake me for a kid, Shermie. What's going on there that you needed me or my dad?" Shermie explained to him what had happened and then what the nurse had said. Then he explained how Mr. Coldwell couldn't get in touch with his mom or grandparents. "So you're being bullied there, are you?"

"Yes, sir." He started crying again and told Mr. Strong he was sorry. "I know that I'm supposed to be like a big person, but my head hurts."

"Have you told your mom what's going on there?" He said that he didn't want to add to her stress; she was very stressed out all the time. "I understand. I'm on my way. And since my dad is on the school board there, I'll bring him along with me. We'll get you taken care of, all right?"

"Yes, sir. Thank you." After telling him what school he was going to as well as where he was, Mr.

B, what he was going to call Barton Strong from now on, said he was on his way. Shermie started to lay back down with the now warm ice pack, but his belly churned up, and he sat up and hurried to the bathroom. He didn't make it.

Nearly passing out on the floor after his belly emptied, Shermie laid on the cool floor while the kids in the hall walked around him. Two of the bullies he was having trouble with kicked him, and Shermie just wanted to die. He hurt all over.

"What have you done? Didn't I tell you to be still?" Shermie looked up at the nurse and told him that he didn't tell him anything. "Well, you should have stayed where you were. Now there is puke all over the floor, and you're going to have to clean it up. Your mother should have trained you better than to just puke where you—oh my goodness, you have it all over yourself. Well, you're going to have to wear that home. We don't have extra clothing around for kids that think they're smarter than—"

"Shermie?" He was never so glad to hear a man's voice than he was at that moment. Mr. B. picked him up off the floor and held him to his body. No matter how many times he told him he was messy, he held him all the tighter. "Did you call an ambulance for this head wound?"

"If I had to call an ambulance for every time a kid hit his head, then they'd be lined up all around the school. He's faking it. He just wants to get out of class. Besides, when I asked him if he wanted one, he told me no, didn't you Sherman?" Too sick to think that something wasn't right, he shook his head when Mr. B. asked him about it, too. "He's lying. What else do you expect a little boy to do when he's been caught faking an injury to go home to his mommy."

Shermie didn't know what happened, but he knew that Mr. Coldwell had passed out or something. He was slumped against the wall when Mr. B. picked him up in his arms. Sick again, he whispered in his ear that he needed to puke again, and he was rushed to the bathroom. Making it this time, Shermie was ever so happy that he'd been given Mr. B's phone number when they'd had dinner together last week. He was his hero.

After being put in the ambulance, he reminded Mr. B. that he had puke to clean up. When his dad, Mr. B., too, he only just realized, asked him who had said that to him, and he said that the nurse had. Then he asked what had happened to the other man.

"He got smart with the wrong person." The

younger Mr. B. leaned to his ear and told him that his dad had knocked the man on his ass for treating him that way. "My dad isn't going to let things like this happen again."

Barton, as he was asked to call him—and boy was Shermie glad for that, rode with him to the hospital. On the way there, he held onto his hand because they had put a collar on his neck and a gauzy-like cloth on his face. Having a hand to hang onto didn't make him scared as much. It was Barton who got ahold of his mom.

"My dad is taking care of the school on how he was treated. He told Shermie that he had tried to contact you and your parents, but after meeting the man, I don't think he tried at all. It was Shermie who called me. I hope that's all right?" His mom must have said it was all right because the small squeeze to his hand made him feel like he didn't do anything wrong. "The medics here are saying that he's going to need a few stitches and that he'll more than likely have to spend a night in the hospital. Dad is going to get the recordings of what really happened so that if you wish, you can press charges."

"You're going to feel a small pinch, Shermie, all right?" He nodded, then remembered that no one could see him well and told the person he thought it was another nurse with him, and it was all right. Almost as soon as he said ouch to the pain, he didn't feel another thing. "There you go, son. Let the medication work for you, and you'll not feel a thing."

Things were fading in and out for him for a while after that. He heard Barton talking to someone once. Then he said that the police were there. Even when he heard his mom's voice, he couldn't seem to make his mouth work. Grandda was there, too. He held his hand and told him he was a brave boy at one point.

"Shermie? Shermie, can you hear me?" His mouth was as dry as their yard was one year when they'd not watered it for a few days. Trying to talk, tell whoever it was that he was there when he laughed. "There you are. My name is Doctor Cunningham. I'm a good friend of the Strong family. They asked for you to get the best care, and I'm going to be your doctor. Do you have any questions for me before we take you up to your room?"

"Mom here?" He said that she was eating with Barton while he was being moved. "My head is starting to hurt again. Will it ever stop?"

"I'm going to give you just a little more juice

to put you under. Don't fight it, young man. Just let it go over you so that you can rest and heal faster." He said that he would. "Good man. You don't worry about a thing. I've got—" That was the last thing that he heard before his body just went to sleep.

Chapter 3

Toria was glad now that it had been the Strongs that
had gone to the school when Shermie needed them.
She would have, no doubt, fallen apart, and that
wouldn't have done anyone any good. Especially
her son. Even now that it was ten days past, she still
found herself getting up in the middle of the night to
check on him.

The three boys that had knocked her son around
were in jail. As all of them were eighteen years old,
they had been considered adults and chargeable with
his being hurt and bullied. Also, the school nurse,
as well as the principal, were sitting inside the jail
cells for their parts in the trouble Shermie had been
having. She didn't yet understand why the principal
had been arrested, but the boys had caused Shermie
to have forty-three stitches in his forehead and ten in

the back of his head when he'd fallen backward and hit his head a second time.

The nurse, Mr. Coldwell, had been arrested for child endangerment because he'd denied her son the proper care, and he didn't call her when he said that he had. Toria didn't know what the charges were actually called, but she knew that he had a long list of other incidents with other children, including more things with Shermie that she'd not been aware of. Shermie was now recuperating at home, and she was trying to work through not just her anger but also her guilty feelings of not being there when he needed her.

However, it was good that Barkley was on the school board, or there was no telling how long Shermie and other kids who were just trying to get through their day would have continued being bullied daily would have gone on. Stretching out her neck caused it to pop twice and drew the attention of her dad.

"You're working too hard, baby." She told him that she had a lot going on. "Not enough that you're stressed like this all the time. Did you fire that secretary yet?"

"I can't do it, Dad. She has a family to provide

for." Dad told her that wasn't her problem as the woman was incompetent and needed to be replaced before anything else happened at work. "I know. I just can't seem to get up…she has a grandson that she's raising that is the same age as Shermie."

"No, she doesn't." As Barton entered the office where she was working, he handed her a file. "My dad did a background check on her. Well, all your staff. It's sort of required since my brother is running for Congress. Ms. Blanchard is a single woman who not only gets help from the government — they too were told that she has children that depend on her — three as a matter of fact, but she has also filed with the office that she's only making about half what you pay her. Dad is taking care that she's caught."

"While I thank you for doing this, why are *you* doing this? I mean, they're my staff." She didn't much care for Barton. He was a fucking pushy bastard. If not for Shermie liking him, she would have been finished with him weeks ago. He told her again about his brother. "I'm well aware that your brother is running. His name is all over town in yards. But what I'm asking you is why didn't you tell me to do it? I would have, you know."

"Yes, but as your son and father tell you all the

time, you're stressed enough as it is." She was frankly sick of people pointing out how stressed she was all the time, too. "Which brings me to the second reason that I'm here. Your grannie is going on a cruise the day after tomorrow. Were you aware of that? Also, she's taking you with her so that you can't come into the office all hours of the night to work on projects that have enough of a headway in finishing up before the deadline. Your sister was invited. To be honest with you, I didn't know you had one, but she said that she was still mad at you and wouldn't be stuck on a boat with you even…well, I think you can imagine what she said. My mom is going too with my sister's-in-laws to have some fun." She stood up, ready to do battle with him.

"Toria, I did this." Turning to look at her dad, she was surprised that he backed away from her. "Don't. Don't lose your temper with me, Victoria Davies. I'm your father, and I'm worried about you. Now, please sit down. I've had to battle your sister today, and I've had just about enough of my daughters to tell you the truth." She sat down. However, she wasn't at all happy with anyone. It was Barton who explained how she'd come to be going on an unwanted cruise with her grannie.

"Your father called my dad last night. He and Dad were talking, and your dad mentioned that his mom was going on a cruise for two weeks with his wife. Dad was told how she took these trips a couple of times a year to reset herself. Victoria told him that it makes her feel like she can go on when she returns, and nothing bothers her. Also, she told him that it's a wonderful way to get your head out of the office." She told Barton and her dad that she didn't want to go on a cruise. "The tickets have already been purchased. Your mom packed the things that you were going to need up, and our plane is going to take the bunch of you to Florida so that you can be there first thing that morning to leave."

"I'm not going." Her dad asked if he could talk to her alone. "It won't do you any good to talk to me alone or with fifty people, Dad. I don't want to go. I have stuff to do that is up to my eyeballs and—"

"Damn it, Victoria, I can't lose you." When her dad burst into tears before anyone could leave her office, she looked at Barton when he sat down beside her dad. "Do you know what I feel every time I see you? Like I'm failing you. You remember your grandfather, don't you? Good lord, he was, if you can believe it, less stressed than you are right now, and he had a massive stroke one day at work. You're killing yourself. And I don't mean that as a joke. You're literally killing yourself right before my eyes. Right in front of your son's eyes. Did you know that he calls me nightly to tell me how worried he is about you? That he doesn't tell you half the stuff that is going on in his — he is stressing out, too. Thanks to you. Are you this willing to work this hard to leave us all when you have a massive stroke like my father did? Go on the fucking cruise. Drink too much. Eat until you pop. But please go and not worry about a damned thing while gone but what you should be wearing to dinner that night."

Dad sobbed, and when she went to him on bended knee to give him comfort, he pulled her into his arms and held her as he cried on her shoulder. Toria had never felt so helpless — this was the second time she'd felt this way in her entire life as she did at that moment. She'd hurt her father. They were leaving her no choice but to go. It was go or have her dad upset with her. And her son.

"All right, Dad. I'll go. I'll pack up and go with the ladies on this cruise." Dad was nodding, but he was still crying. It was like she was having her heart ripped out with every noise he made. "I don't, however, think that Shermie will want to go. He hates the water and will never, I don't think, set his foot on the ship for fear of it sinking right there in the harbor."

She'd been going for a joke, but she failed so badly. Dad held onto her as he mopped his face with one of the napkins on the table that had been set up in the conference room. When she sat in the chair in front of her dad, Barton was pulling one over so she could get up off her knees. Toria thanked him but held her father's hand.

"If Shermie doesn't want to go, he can stay with me. I can make sure that he's fed and clothed." She said that her dad would see to him. But she did thank him. "All right. If they need any help, my entire family will be there for the two of them. If that's all right with you. To be honest, my Aunt, my dad's sister, has the same fear of water. Aunt Piper had to be taken off the ship at an emergency harbor landing her first trip out to sea."

At a little after noon, she was home going through the luggage that her mom had packed for her. She'd done well, Toria thought, trying not to feel like she'd been blackmailed into this trip when she really did have a lot of things going on. One of them was the hiring of a secretary who wouldn't lie to her about having a child.

Toria wanted Shermie to tell her that he couldn't live without her for two weeks when she told him where she was going. Instead, he told her how much fun he was going to have hanging out with his grandda and Mr. Strong. All the Strongs, he told her. And getting to go to the manor every day. She had to ask what Manor he was talking about, and she was surprised—just a little, anyway, that he meant the Strong Manor. Apparently, them just getting two baby goats was better entertainment than talking to her. However, as soon as she saw the kids, she fell in love with them too.

"You'll see, we'll come back so refreshed and feeling good that you won't want to go back to work." She smiled at her grannie and hugged her. "You've no idea how many times that I wanted to kidnap you and take you with me. And now we're going, and I'm beside myself with happiness."

"I don't know, Grannie. I might just be a stick in the mud, and you'll wish you'd never invited me." Grannie told her *fizzle sticks*. She'd not heard her say that in a long time. Smiling at her grannie, she told her about her lack of trips. "I've never been anywhere, you know. Not even when my class went on school trips did I go with them. I honestly don't remember ever having a vacation since Shermie was born."

"You need to get yourself laid, too." Toria looked at her grandmother until she reached over and closed her mouth. "Do you think that your father just appeared in a crib one afternoon while I was home? No, dear, your grandda and I had lots of sex making your father."

"That is entirely too much information. If you don't mind, please don't share those things with me again." They were both laughing when they were getting out of the car at the department store. "I only need a few things to take with me. You didn't have to come, too. In and out of the store, and I'll be finished."

"We're going shopping, Toria. You and I are going to spend an ungodly amount of money today, and I'm going to make sure that you are having fun, too. Then the other ladies are going to meet us at that lovely little restaurant to have our first of many meals together. And try very hard to look like you're having fun. I do believe that your mother is reporting back to your father on how many times you smile."

She did smile then. "There's my girl. I knew that you had a smile or two there someplace. I do love you, my dear, but you have become a stick in the mud. We're all going to get rid of that confounded stick and show you how to have a wonderful time. I do believe you've forgotten how."

By the time she and her grannie made their way to the place they were eating, she was exhausted. Her feet hurt, too. But she had to admit, she was looking forward to this trip more than she could have imagined. Even buying herself some nice sun dresses, something that she'd never worn before, excited her a great deal. Thinking of the warmth of the sun touching her shoulder, she found that she couldn't smash her excitement by even thinking of work.

~*~

Barton looked over the table and chairs while keeping an eye out for his dad and Warren. They had decided last night that they were going to buy the homestead that was being auctioned off at noon today. Dad wanted to purchase it for the new adventure that he was thinking of, and Warren said that he had it in mind to renovate and restore. Dad joined him in that idea, and the two of them were now in business together, it seemed.

"Hello, Barton." He was down on his knees when Shermie came up to him and spoke. Asking for his help, the little boy was more than happy to crawl under the table and tell him what he saw. "It does have a label on it. And, like you said, the locks are all rusty, but I can knock it off. There's a mechanism under here, too, with a crank. What me to move it?"

"Not yet. Come out before someone sees you." Shermie came out from under the table and asked if he'd be in trouble if caught. "Not at all. I would have had to crawl under there to see what you saw for me, and I wouldn't have been unnoticed like you are. See, this is a very old table that is worth a great deal of money. Or it will be once I clean it up. Now, let me ask you a couple of questions. Was the mechanism wood or metal? And was the crank wood or metal?"

"Both were wood. And there was a little knob thing on the handle of the crank that looked like it was made from a big marble." Barton felt excitement race over his skin. He could tell that Shermie was getting in on it, too, when he moved closer to him and whispered. "Also, the label looks like it's made from handmade paper. And then nailed, not stapled to the table. How about I use your phone to take a picture of it, and that way, I can show you what I saw?"

The two of them looked around at the other people before Shermie slipped under the table, did his job, and came back to standing next to him in a minute. Barton looked at the picture with him and discovered that the handle had been topped with a large cat's eye marble. Something that he'd never seen done before. He and Shermie whispered about it for the rest of the morning while looking around. Barton also let him know the rules about buying and bidding. Barton hadn't looked forward to an auction in a very long time as much as he did today.

His dad had his heart set on a colonial bedroom suite. After employing Shermie to look around the piece for several minutes, Barton thought that he couldn't have had a better partner to help them out. Handing him his phone when he asked for it, he didn't mind at all when he came back to him excited for his own find.

"I've always wanted a big trunk in my room for my special things. I don't know anything about it, but that it's huge." His excitement for the trunk was contagious, and when they all followed him to where it was, Barton could see that it was in good shape.

Even the leather handles were still in tack, but it was about as filthy as anything that he'd ever seen. "The man over there, he told me that it had been sitting in the barn since he was a little boy. He said for me not to open the trunk until I buy it. He seemed pretty sure that I'd be the only one that would bid on it."

"Did he say not to open it or that you couldn't open it?" Dad leaned down to Shermie, pretending to tie his shoe when he asked him. "If there is a key to it, this will be a nice treasure trunk for you."

"He gave me the key when we were talking." Dad looked at him, and then Shermie turned to him, too. "If you would bid on it for me, Barton, I'll pay you back whatever you have to pay. I want this really bad. I think even my mom would like me to have it."

"You can bid on it." He shook his head and said he'd never done it before. "You've been watching everyone around here bid. You know the rules, right? Set yourself a price you're willing to pay, don't look at other people and breathe. That's the one I used to forget to do when I first started out. You got this. I know you can do it."

After Shermie got the assurances that he needed, they headed back over to the beginning of the furniture lots. Dad and Warren headed to the box lots with Shermie so that he could practice. Even if Shermie didn't go as high as the bids were coming in, Barton was going to get the trunk for him for helping them out today. At around noon, after he successfully got the table and chairs as well as the two other pieces that went with it for a very good price, he made his way over to Dad to see what he did about getting the house for a good price.

"Barton, do you think that I could get something to eat? I have money." Barton assured him that he was hungry, too, and they made their way to the food truck while his dad was listening to the specs on the house. "I'm super nervous for your dad and didn't want to let my excitement mess it up for him. Do you think that they'll get it?"

"I don't know why not. Dad is the one who taught me how to bid and win. Mom loves to go, too. She gets things like hankies and pretty antimacassars to sell online." After telling him what an antimacassar was, Shermie laughed. "I'm not kidding you. Men used to wear a lot of products in their hair that would ruin chair backs, so women would make them so that they could keep their furniture nice looking."

"I guess that makes sense. We kinda need one for the whole couch sometimes when I'm being messy. I try hard not to be, but I forget when I'm watching something exciting on television." Barton ruffled his hair and told Shermie that he did the same thing. "Yeah, last night when we were watching the game, you did get a lot messy."

They stood under a large tree and ate two hot dogs each, and then Shermie enjoyed a piece of chocolate cake. Still off sweets, he got an apple from the woman who was cutting them up to fry with the onions and peppers for the sausages she was selling too. Shermie and he headed to the box lots again to see where they were in the line. It looked like they were about halfway done when Shermie found something in a box that excited him immensely.

"My mom would love that pendant. It's her favorite stone. Dark rubies." Neither of them reached into the box to see if it was flawed or not, but Barton told Shermie that if he could get it for a few bucks, they could have it cleaned up. "I'm going to do it."

When the box before the one that the kid wanted was being bid on, he was proud of the kid, watching how he kept an eye on the people bidding and not the box. When it didn't sell, the auctioneer added four more boxes to the one to 'sweeten the deal,' including the one that Shermie wanted. Barton was happy that Shermie didn't give up on his need for the single box but did bid on the lot of them and won it all for a buck. He didn't know who was more excited, Shermie or the people surrounding him. After dragging all the boxes to the tree where they'd been stashing their small purchases, Shermie went right back to see if he could win anything else of the jewelry that looked as if it had been dumped out of the drawers and brought out.

After helping Shermie with his loot, the two of them went back to the furniture. Barton had already made a call to have one of his brothers rent a large truck to take some of the larger pieces. His dad and Warren had gotten some items as well, so he was happy that he'd not have to lug things home by himself. They were back in plenty of time for the trunk to be auctioned off. And while they'd been gone, there had been several other pieces — in addition to four more trunks added to the line.

"We've located another stash of box lots, ladies and gentlemen. Mr. Wells, the family that is having this auction, forgot about the overhead storage in the barn. If you've not had an opportunity to look over the new things, please do so now. We'll be there to have bids brought in in just a little while.

Maybe five minutes." The auctioneer looked a little frazzled. Shermie asked him if he was all right. "I am. Just...I don't like it when they don't let us know in time about pieces that could bring in some money. Having them remember something like these boxes of items might have brought someone here who would want them. Now, we'll not get the price that we might well have."

Shermie, of course, didn't understand that, so he explained it to him with the help of his dad. When they saw people looking the new items over, he wasn't surprised to watch them walk away. Everything in the pile, as many as a dozen boxes and a few more trunks that were covered in mouse poop and dirt, looked like they might well have just been saved from the dumpster rather than something that might be a good find.

"No one is opening the boxes up to see what's in them." He told Shermie that was normal. "So they're just going to bid on it without knowing what they get? That seems silly, don't you think?"

"No. If they don't know what's in them, it'll be like a surprise of fun for them when they get them home. If they don't pay too much. Say you get one of them for five bucks, and you find out you have a lot of old books in the box. Then you didn't get a great deal because very few people collect old books. But, if you get it for the same price and you find that it's filled with vintage clothing or old toys, you made out very well. It's the thrill of it, Shermie, not usually getting a great deal. To me and my family, at least." Shermie understood, and Barton could tell the exact moment that it hit Shermie that he could buy something just because he wanted it and not for a reason. "You understand the thrill now, don't you?"

"Yes." His grin was infectious, and when his dad and Warren joined them, having not won the house because someone didn't understand bidding but they weren't unhappy. "Did someone just take the first bid that the man put out there? Barton said that's the mark of a newbie."

"Yes, he did, as a matter of fact. He paid well over double for the house had he just waited on bidding." Dad, having done it to all of them when they'd been children, ruffled Shermie's hair. "You're a good kid, young man. It's been a pleasure hanging out with you today. And I think you did a great job for us, too."

When the bidding opened up with the new items, the auctioneer looked a little deflated when no one but them came to the area but he and his family. Not even the person who was writing down what was sold to which bidder number looked all that thrilled. Putting his hand on his hip, he asked Shermie, who had his number in his front pocket, what he might want to bid on in the pile.

"I was thinking about what might be in those boxes. Could it be a treasure? Could it be a dud? I don't know, but I'd like to see what's in them for a story to tell my mom when she comes back from vacation." He asked Shermie if Barton was his father. "No, sir. But if there was ever one that could be, I think he would be perfect. But my momma, she just, well, I think she likes arguing with him. Seems to make them both happy."

"Sherman." His family turned to him, and Barton could feel his face heat up in embarrassment. "While I appreciate your honesty, why don't you tell this man what it is you want to bid so we can get to treasure hunting. All right?"

Shermie told the auctioneer that he'd give him ten dollars for all that was left behind. His wording of it had the auctioneer thinking he meant the entire area, not just the stuff that they were standing by. His looking around at what was left behind confirmed it.

Some of the things were big items that either they decided were too large for traveling or they didn't have the help they thought they might for picking it up. Either way, it would end up in a dumpster, or someone would take it home for their barn. After looking around at what people were leaving after paying for things, Barton and Dad thought that he'd made a good deal.

"Mr. Strong? Mr. Barkley Strong?" Dad and Shermie were looking through one of the boxes, having found that he'd hit a dud on the first try and was flagged down by Mr. Bailey, the auctioneer. "I just spoke to Mr. Cramer. He purchased the house. He told me that he'd made a mistake in buying it, paying too much. I'm betting he didn't secure his loan before coming here today. Mr. Cramer is willing to forfeit the house and what he put down on it if you'd like to buy the house from him. He, as you know, the buyer had to have half the purchase price as a hold for ninety days until he could secure a house loan. His banker turned him down already."

Dad looked at him and Warren for a few minutes. Barton knew that his dad was calculating in his head. When he asked to be able to go through the house, he nearly kissed his father. After touring the house with Shermie just after having lunch with Shermie, he had been going to ask his dad if he could buy it from him. It was a beautiful antebellum of a home.

The four of them looked over the house from top to bottom. Mr. Bailey had given them the specs on the house, and Barton was surprised to find out that it had had a new roof put on last fall and a new furnace and air conditioning put in at that time, too. Dad was ready to buy it when he took him aside and asked him if he could.

"You know, when I first got here today, I thought that this would be the perfect place for you. Did you happen to go in the basement, son? There is a very nice wine cellar as well as an outside entrance if you wanted to use that too." He told him his plans for the house. "Your mother will love that you're going to bring the gardens back. I'm sure she'll help you, but another thing is that you'll be within walking distance to your office and the others' homes."

"I saw that too," Dad told him that it had several acers on either side of the house that were for sale by the owner. "Good to know. I'm going to work on owning that, too, if I can."

"Make sure you have someone else buying it

for you." They had learned that there were people who would take advantage of a sale if they knew that the Strongs were wanting it. He'd lost a lot of deals, having to walk away when they found out it was him purchasing something and jacked up the prices. "The house is going to be in your name, so I'd find someone to do it soon before things get around."

"I'll use Toria's firm to purchase it for me. It won't seem suspicious if she brokers the deal for me, would it?" Dad said it was a good idea, but it was Warren who said he'd do it for Barton. "Thank you. I really appreciate that, Warren."

"I bet you don't sell the table and chairs now, do you? Those sure will look pretty in that dining room now." Barton agreed with Shermie. They made their way to Mr. Bailey to let him know that he was going to buy it, and Warren asked for the person selling off the land next to the house."

"It'll come to you, too, Mr. Strong. Mr. Crabapple, the man in charge of the estate, told me when he got what he had hoped for, the things like the boxes and furniture that I could just throw it in. I didn't tell Mr. Cramer. Not that I was hiding it from him, but I only just found out when I went to tell Crabapple what had happened. I was supposed to come to you rather than going back to the realtor after the sale went downhill. I hope that was all right and you didn't feel like I forced you into the sale or anything." Dad assured him that he didn't feel that way at all. "Good. Good then. Barton, you've five hundred acres to go with the house. There is a barn too about a mile from here up the road that is part of the homestead, too. You got yourself a good deal today if you don't mind me saying so. A good place to have a family, too. Thank you all for coming today."

After he walked away, Barton waited until he was out of sight before he did a dance around the yard. Christ, he was thrilled. And when Shermie asked him if he could have a room in his new home, he picked the kid up and hugged him tightly.

"You can, as a matter of fact." The four of them, with the help of his brothers, helped load the things they'd gotten back in the house. Since he'd gotten the key, he figured that it would be the best place to sort through all of it, too. They all heard Shermie scream in what was going to be his bedroom ten minutes after they'd gotten the dining room furniture set back in the room.

Chapter 4

Toria was as excited as her son was about what had been in the trunk he'd gotten today. As he showed her all the boxes and envelopes of change, she wished again that she'd been there when he'd opened it. It was a hell of a find for a six-year-old.

"Mr. Crabapple came by the house after I yelled. I did scream like a little girl, Barton told me, and scared fifty years off his life. Grandda too. He said that when I found something important, it would save all their lives if I would politely come and find him and calmly tell him that I'd found something in one of the trunks." He looked at her on the telephone he was using to talk to her face-to-face. "Mom, Mr. Crabapple said that he and his wife would put the change they'd had left over every day in an envelope or box, whatever they could find at the time, and put it in the trunk. Even if they needed something extra, they never touched that money. I'm going take it to the bank a little at a time, so I don't give myself a hernia like Barkley said, carrying the trunk on my back. He sure is a nice man. He told me what a hernia is, too."

"I bet he did." She watched as he put the trunk against the wall and pulled a large box to him. "Are we going to open another one?"

He'd taken a few of the boxes that had been sealed up from the auction to her dad's home to open. Setting up a cell phone so that they could open them together was the best surprise that she could have shared with him. So far, they'd only opened the one, another dud, she was told, but his excitement about what might be in the next one was hard to contain. Forever the optimist he was.

"Okay, here we go." The box, he told her, wasn't all that heavy, but he could hear glass being shook around. Barton joined him in his bedroom, there to keep him from being cut on glass, and they told her about the house that Barton had purchased. "It's a big old house, Mom. You're going to love all the secret places in it that Mr. Crabtree told us about."

"I'm sure that Mr. Strong wants to keep those

secret, too." The tape was cut through, and she heard Barton whistle. "What did you get, Shermie?"

"Oh, Mom, they're beautiful. Ornaments. The kind you like with glitter and stuff all over them." When he pulled the top box out carefully, she could see, of any glass that might be on them. He put the box up to let her see. "Oh, Mom, there are so many of them. And they're so colorful." Barton spoke next.

"These are very old. I'd say from the last century, at least. You could sell them and get a bit of money or keep them and use them for your own tree. If you decide to sell them, my mom would love to see them." Toria said that it was Shermie's find and his decision on what he wanted to do with them. Unless he borrowed the money to purchase them. "We paid him for the day by getting what he wanted, so that's all taken care of. The kid is a natural at auctions. He helped us out a great deal by scoping things out. That's very good of you to allow him to decide. You should be proud of him, too."

"I am. Forever proud of him. And thank you for keeping an eye on him while I'm away. My dad said he'd forgotten how energic a six-year-old boy could be." Shermie was ready to open the next box. She was sure that he was embarrassed about them talking about him. When the camera was at the next box, she watched as her son carefully cut open the box with a sharp-looking box knife. "Be careful, buddy."

"I am, Mom. I have something that I want to —" Barton told him to focus on one thing at a time while using a sharp object. "All right. I forgot."

Good advice, she thought. She needed to do that more in her life, too. When he got the box open, she watched as he carefully pulled out the loose newspaper off the top. Barton read the date of the newspapers as he set them aside for Shermie. Shermie said it would be fun to read the news written on them. She couldn't wait to spend an afternoon doing that very thing with him.

This box was filled with lots of paper and rags. However, whatever it was seemed to be wrapped up tightly in newspaper, and then cloth pieces that looked to have been old dish towels had been used to separate the layers, Shermie told her. When he got the first one unwrapped, Barton whistled. Shermie just stared at whatever he had in his hand.

"You're making me nervous. Tell me what it is." The women entered her room and she explained what she was doing. Her mom sat next to her to see

Shermie when he held up the item in his hand. "It looks like another ornament. Is that right?"

"It's a glass ornament. I would say hand-blown, too. It's beautiful. Can you see the design?" She couldn't, so it was Barton who held it up to the camera for her and Mom. It was a fig, he told her. "This is very old. I'd say that it's from Lauscha, Germany's Thuringian Forest. The first blown ornaments were crafted there in the sixteenth century. I'm not sure if these are that old, but they're very old." She told him the same thing as before, that it would be Shermie's decision.

"I'll buy them from him. All the ornaments." She told Barton that he didn't have to do that. "No, I don't. But these will make wonderful Christmas gifts for my family. Old-world things like this would be a great hit. And whatever is left over, if I do go that route, I can have the most expensive tree decorations of all time. But I do love these. This is the only one that we've pulled out, and I know that the others will be just as beautiful."

Barton and Shermie pulled out the rest of the boxes' inventory. The ornaments kept getting more and more beautiful with each one they unwrapped. At the bottom of the box, there were three wooden boxes that were sealed up with a small hook closure. Shermie pulled them out and sat them on the floor so that she could see that they were beautifully carved boxes, too. She wanted to come through the phone and hurry him along in opening them.

"I don't know what these are, but I'm going to save it for my new friends and grandpa Warren to have. Whatever it is, I know that they'll like it, and it will be a great thank you for the two grandpas that were with me today and Barton." Shermie looked at her. "That's what I wanted to ask you. Barkley has been like a grandpa to me, and I'd like to call him that if it's all right with you, Mom. And Barton has been like a dad to me, so much that I think you're telling him how to keep me focused when I get overly excited. They didn't treat me like some kid they had to hang out with but like a real person."

"You are a real person, Shermie." She watched as he hugged Barton for saying that to him. Her mom and Grannie walked away on her end to get tissues; they were both crying. Even Lisa was wiping away the tears she had shed. "If it's all right with your mom, I'm sure that my dad will be over the moon with you calling him that."

"I think it's a grand idea. But it would be, as

Barton said to you, up to you, Toria. My goodness, I'm so emotional right now I think I'd better take a little walk." Her mom joined Lisa as they pulled on their sweaters. The two of them had been hanging out together since they boarded three days ago. "I'll meet you ladies in the dining room. I'm ready to eat until I pop."

When the door closed behind the two women, the others left as well. It was just her and Barton with Shermie. But Barton said that he was going to do some searches on the ornaments so he could give Shermie a good price if he was ready to sell them. She looked at her son as he moved the boxes to the end of his bed.

"Are you all right, Mom? I meant to ask you if you're having fun. You sure do look like you're tanning right up." She told him that she'd been relaxing by the pool today and might have gotten a little burnt. And that she was having a very good time. "I'm so glad. You even look like you're relaxed, too. Grandda is going into the offices in the morning, then he's home to spend the day with us after lunch. Grandpa Warren goes to his office, but he said it was just to make sure that his sons are working. Everybody here has been so nice to me so far."

"Why wouldn't they? I raised you perfectly." They both laughed. "Yesterday, Grandma and I had lunch in the big dining room. The food was so good. You and I will have to go on a trip soon after I get back. Maybe on a train or something."

"I'd like that. Barton and his brothers are helping me get over the fear of water that I have. Yesterday, I was able to sit on the edge with my feet dangling. Maverick told me that it would take little steps to get over my fear, and if anyone tells me differently or that I'm silly for being afraid, I was to tell him. He'd make sure they were afraid of something too, he told me." Shermie laughed. "They're like having bodyguards with me all the time. I love them all. And they say that back to me, too. Even giving me lots of hugs."

"I'm glad that you're having so much fun too." She wanted to caution him on being too close to them but didn't want to spoil his fun. He really did look like he was having the best time with each thing that he told her he'd been up to. "You're getting to school on time, too, aren't you?"

"I forgot to tell you. They closed the school down. Since it was almost summer break, they said it would take them a while to have the police go over the videos that they were given, so we couldn't go anyway." She asked what he'd heard about that. "Grandpa Warren is on the board, and he told grandda and me that they had to fire most of the teachers as they were doing wrong to kids, too. One of the teachers had a gun in their desk drawer. She told the police that she wasn't going to be killed because kids are so rotten nowadays. That was scary to me."

"Me too. My goodness. I had no idea." Shermie told her that he'd not either but was glad that they were going to hire new teachers for the fall. "My dad sent me some links for some private schools that Barkley did a search about. When I get home, you and I will read over the information and see what you'd like to do. I don't want you to be bullied or hurt again."

"I'm going to be hurt no matter what, Mom. You know that. But I was talking to Jenson—he's been super nice to me, too, but he said that he and his brothers were homeschooled by their mother and others until they got to high school. Grandpa B said if you want, he can help you find someone to teach me at home. I've been thinking about that, too." Feeling overwhelmed again, she changed the subject and asked him about his plans now that school was out. "The Grandpas have to go to Columbus tomorrow for a meeting, like I said. That is going to take all the morning and into the afternoon. I'm going to stay with Barton, and we're going to find something to get into at his new house. I told you that he bought the Crabapple estate, didn't I?"

"Yes, you did. I loved that old place. Is he going to modernize it all up? That would be such a shame if you ask me." She could see Barton doing something like that. Getting rid of the old and making it all chrome and glass. Toria was so deep in thought that she missed what Shermie had said. "I'm sorry, honey. What did you just say?"

"I said that he's bringing the old girl back to life. That's what he called it, anyway. The day that he bought it, he also got the dining room table and the chairs. I guess there were these two pieces that matched it that had to be stripped down and cleaned up. The movers that were taking it to their repair shop found that it was stuffed full of China and silverware that they'd found stuck in the corner that hadn't sold either. Like the original things that had been in the house that no one wanted. The dishes have a painting on them of the big barn that is up the road. We're going to go there soon too to see what's in it. Everything has the barn on it, I guess. It's a lot of plates and stuff like vases and girly stuff like that." She asked him why he thought it was girly stuff, trying hard not to laugh. "The cups and saucers are little bitty things. You couldn't get much hot cocoa in them. And there are a bunch of flower vases, too. About a dozen candle holders, too. Barton told me that it was probably because the room would have been so dark without overhead lights that you would have needed a bunch of candles. It has lights in there now. That's the only thing that had to be done to that room, but the windows and floor cleaned up. I like that room a lot, too."

They talked for about another ten minutes before he said that he needed some sleep. He also told her that he had a big day tomorrow and would probably be exhausted tomorrow since he was going to be working with Barton. When she closed the connection a few minutes later after telling him how much she loved him, Toria left her room to go join the others, thinking about how deeply she and Shermie had come to depend on the Strongs.

It was going to end badly. She knew this not just for her son but for her as well. Toria hadn't planned on falling in love with having a girls' vacation. She was sure had it been anyone else, people that she knew better than the women she was with now, it wouldn't have been at all as much fun as she was having. Even her mom told her that they couldn't have picked better people for their first cruise.

All the women had a good sense of humor. Jade, who was scary smart, didn't talk over her head. She didn't offer up advice either unless someone asked her. Being a doctor and a mechanical engineer made for great stories that she'd tell. The one she loved the most was how she'd ended up meeting Jenson, her husband. Then there was the story of how she was raising her mother's son. They all had delightful stories that they told her about.

Sitting at the table with them, she was glad to see that they'd ordered her a salad. Since she was a child, she would have a big salad before each meal so that she would not eat too much of the high-calorie part of the meal. She noticed that Carrie, Barkley's wife, did the same thing.

"I've been meaning to ask you about Shermie. He's mentioned a couple of times that he was kidnapped when he was four years old. There wasn't anything in the paper about him. I'm assuming that is right because he was a child, but what happened?" Lizzy, Clay's wife, then told her that she didn't have to tell them if she didn't want to. "It's just something that I was curious about. No biggie if you don't want to tell."

"I don't mind." Glancing at her mom and grannie, she cleared her throat before starting. "It's why Shermie won't have anything to do with waterways. Only that. Not all water. He'll take a bath, but he'll not get into a pool or boat that sits on the shore, even."

Toria had told the story so many times to the police when it had first happened that she knew all the details in order, as well as the things that had been done to her son. Looking around the table as their meals were set before them, she was going to tell them because it was important to her that people knew his story and not to make fun of him.

"My husband, Sherman, died sixteen months after we were married. It was a hell of a blow when we found out that he had an inoperable form of cancer on our honeymoon. He'd fallen while getting out of the limo we were in and had been rushed to the hospital for his broken ankle. While there, blood tests were run, and a scan of his ankle revealed that he had bone cancer as well. We were on our honeymoon, so you can imagine what we did next. Flying home so that he could find himself a doctor who would see if the island doctors were right. They were correct. However, instead of him having five years left, he only had five months. Sherman managed to live about a year and a half before he died. By then, I was six months pregnant with Shermie." Everyone told her how sorry they were. "Thank you. So much."

She thought about what had transpired when his parents found out. "Sherman didn't want his parents to know. He'd been estranged from them for ten years by then and didn't want them to know he was dying now that he was sick. I didn't contact them. I didn't know how, but one of the nurses on staff figured out who Sherman was related to and called them herself."

"I would have taken her to the cleaners over that." Toria told Jade that by the time she'd figured out who had called them, Sherman was in the final days of his life. "So they were there when he passed away."

"Not the day he passed away. No one but myself was at his side. I had to get a restraining order against them because they were making life-changing changes about his life that Sherman nor I wanted to be done." Her mom told them what one of them was, that they were to resuscitate Sherman so he'd live at all costs. "He didn't want to have tubes and other life-saving techniques done to him. He told me that he wanted to die with dignity. Begged me not to do anything that would prolong his dying on his own terms."

"I take it his family didn't like that. Nor you, I would imagine." She said for a while, they had left her alone. "But then Shermie was born, correct?"

"Yes. And for a few years after his death, things were all right between us. I didn't wholly trust them. I don't know that I ever would have. But over the next few years, three years, they'd come by the house and visit with Shermie. They never spoke about his father, only to say that they'd been to his grave or something like that. Or to tell me how much Shermie looked like their father at that age." She waited again for the waitstaff to leave them before continuing. "Then when Shermie turned four, that day as a matter of fact, they showed their true colors." Mom spoke then.

"We were going to have a celebration. Many of them. Shermie had gotten accepted into a program for the gifted that had been in the works that week. Then, of course, his birthday. I believe there were other things, but for now, I don't...they got into Toria's home and took Shermie. Not only that, but they—oh my, it makes me terrified all over. They had shot Toria six times in the chest and body so that they could take Shermie to raise as their own." Mom hugged her, telling her how much she loved her. As she did every time she told this part of the story. "If not for the neighbor coming over to bring Shermie a gift, Toria might well have died. But the ambulance showed up just as her father and I did."

"Good Christ, that's fucking horrible." Toria had to hide her smile. Jade just said what she thought at times, and while it shocked her at first, she had begun to look forward to it. "I hope these people are in prison someplace. I want to have them still when I go and find them to show them what manners are."

"They're both dead." She nodded like she was glad to hear that but looked disappointed, too. "They had charted a boat for the three of them to leave the country with my son. Shermie fought with them every step of the way, I was told, and when he wouldn't stop screaming...they, they threw him off the boat into the water as a threat for him to stop bringing attention to them and what they were doing. You see, his life jacket, much too large for him, slipped off, and he drown. If not for the quick thinking of the captain, Shermie would have stayed dead. He pulled him from the water with a hook, which hurt him, but as soon as he was coughing and breathing, the captain of the boat pulled out a gun and killed the two of them when they tried to take Shermie from him. He told the police when they got out to the boat what had happened and why he'd shot them, and the men hugged him. My parents did as well when they found out what had happened. The boat captain, his name was Nathan Sams said that he'd been suspicious of them because they were so much older and professing to be the parents to Shermie. He said that he'd had the police on standby as well as he was carrying a gun. Just in case, he said. I didn't meet him until later after I was out of the hospital, but you can bet that I thanked him a great deal, too."

"I think your son is one of the bravest kids I've ever known." Toria agreed with Lizzy and then asked her why she thought so. "He went through a trauma like that one, and still...I was going to say he trusts easily, but I have a feeling that he doesn't. He did, however, trust Barton when he needed help."

"Yes. And I was as surprised by that as I was by anything he's ever done. And he has continued to trust him and this family enough that he's sitting next to the pool and not freaking out." They nodded, all of them. "I don't know about you guys, but I could use a pick me up about now. How about we order desserts and pig out?"

"I love that idea." Jade waved to their server and smiled at him. She was a very beautiful woman, and the man waiting on them looked like he was smitten with her. "I was wondering if we could go to the dessert bar to get a lot of desserts to share?"

"Yes, of course. The kitchen has just replenished the bar, so you will have a large variety of things. May I bring you something to drink too? Tea or coffee?" Jade told them that they'd need both, and he turned so quickly to do what she wanted that he nearly knocked another waiter to the floor.

When he practically ran away from the table, it was her mom who said she felt sorry for the young man. Jade asked her why, and Mom laughed.

"The poor boy will never live this down, for starters, and also, he'll not be back with the coffee and tea. Someone else will do it because he's so embarrassed to show his face again." Jade disagreed, but in the end, her mom was right. A woman brought them their drinks, not saying a word about why she was doing it instead of the young man. But Jade, feeling sorry that the young man had been so embarrassed, made sure that he was given a huge tip to try and make up for him not staying at the table with them.

On her way back to her room, they talked about tomorrow's plans. There was a port of call they were going to, and they all decided to make sure that they left all their valuables on the ship as the captain had suggested. Toria laid out her things to wear so she could get an early start on the morning and laid in bed looking at the pictures that they were all sending them through a family chat. It was pictures of the new baby along with her son too. The other children were there, and she realized that she couldn't tell the family pictures from the children that they'd adopted. It seemed to her that the Strongs treated all the kids equally, including her own. She was just dozing off, not realizing it was so late, until her phone alerted her of a message. It was from Shermie.

"Good night, Mom. I love you so much." There were several emojis along with his message. Then, after sending him one back, he called. "I thought that you'd be asleep by now. I guess you really are having fun."

"Why is it that you're awake, young man? It's nearly midnight." He told her that they'd watched an old movie and had popcorn. "That's wonderful. I'm so glad that you're having time with grandda, Shermie. He must be having a wonderful time with you, too."

"He is. And Grandpa Barkley. They're going to take me to Columbus with them tomorrow to have someone look at the old coins that I found in the trunk. After that, we're going to eat manly stuff all day. Barton is going to have a pool put in the backyard of his new home, and he needs my advice on it." She asked him what sort of advice he thought he could give. "What kind of toys to buy. I told him that he was going to have every one of them if he took me, as I'm a sucker for blow-up things. But he said that with the progress I'm making with sitting at the side, I might be able to stand to get in. He wasn't pushy or anything like that, but I told him that it might be years before I'm that far along. Do you know what he said, Mom? He told me that it didn't matter if I turned ninety-nine before I got in. That was good enough for him. I really love that guy."

After a little bit more talking about his trip to Columbus, the two of them closed the connection. Closing her eyes, Toria thought that she would sleep as well as she had last night because there wasn't a million things on her mind. Maybe, she thought, this vacation thing was good for her. But she was going to wait for a while before she told someone, especially the Strongs, that they'd been right.

Chapter 5

Lorie thought that she'd made her family wait long enough for her to visit them. She wasn't all that happy with any of them, especially her sister, but since she didn't live at home anymore, she seldom saw her. But she was a grown woman, eighteen now, and they should respect her as one. Smiling, she went in the door to her parents' home and moved into the house when their butler told her that dad was having breakfast before he left for the day.

"Where are you going? Not that I really care, Dad. I came to see Mom. Is she sleeping in again?" Lorie had never seen her mom sleep past six in the morning. She didn't usually get up until noon now that she was out of school. Dad told her that Mom was on vacation. "What do you mean, vacation? Where did she go?"

"She went on that cruise with her friends and your sister. I know she told you about it. I believe too that you were invited." Lorie sat down on the chair and stared at her dad. "They left five days ago and have another week to go, I guess."

"But I said that I didn't want to go." Dad nodded at her as he sipped his tea. "She shouldn't have gone there without me. I mean, when I told her that I didn't want to go, that should have meant that she couldn't go either. What does she mean by going on vacation with Victoria and not me."

"Again, Lorie, you were invited and turned it down. You really don't expect your mother not to go simply because you didn't want to go, did you?" She told her father that was exactly what she'd thought. "Don't be so selfish. Your mother and sister are having a wonderful time, and you should be happy for them. I can't believe that you'd think that her decision should be you deciding not to go."

"Well, it should have been. Now, here I am… Victoria talked her into it, didn't she? Just to get back at me for some reason." Dad told her that they'd convinced Toria, not the other way around. "She planned it that way. Just to make me look stupid for staying home. Christ, there are times when I hate

Victoria. I'm guessing that they took her kid, too. He's having a better time than I am on a cruise ship that I didn't get to go on."

"Lorie, what is wrong with you? No, Shermie didn't go. He's afraid of water, as you well know. Not to mention, what would a little boy do on a cruise ship with all of the women." She asked him who had gone with them. "The Strong women. Your grandmother and theirs, I believe. Jade is with them, but her mother, just giving birth, decided to stay home to help Jenson—"

"Blah blah blah. I don't care who went with them. They shouldn't have left me here on my own. Mother should have told me that she was going anyway and that I would have made it so that I'd go too. She tricked me. They both did." Standing up, Lorie asked her dad where he was going. "I mean, I can spend the day with you, I suppose. If you're doing something that I want to do. Otherwise, we'll just stay here and hang out. I'm not going to be dragged all over the place simply because you're bored."

"I'm not bored. And I haven't been since your mom went on her trip. I've been hanging out with the Strongs. They've been helping me entertain Shermie, and we've both been enjoying the things that they do with us." She said she didn't want to go to strangers for entertainment. "That's good because you weren't invited. And you might well not be with the way that you're acting right now. I don't know what you're so upset about all the time, but no one is out to get you, Lorie. And your sister has nothing at all to do with whatever you have in your head that she's done. I frankly don't know why she tries so hard to talk to you. All you've done since her husband died is poke at her." He stared at her for a full minute before he narrowed his eyes at her. "Lorie, please tell me that you had nothing to do with Shermie being kidnapped that day. I'll believe you if you swear that you didn't nearly have your sister killed when they went there to take that little boy from us."

She knew this was going to come out sooner or later, and she had her speech all planned out. It was all her sister's fault for her having to tell them a little lie that made them take Shermie from her. Lorie had been pissed off at her sister because she wouldn't allow her to use her car even though she didn't have a driver's license.

"Dad, you just don't understand how she was treating me. She had all her focus on Shermie and not me. That wasn't right. She was my sister before she was his mom. I just told them that Victoria was going to move to London, and that's all it took. I didn't have anything to do with the planning. And I didn't know that—Dad? Where are you going?" Dad had wiped his mouth off with his napkin and tossed it on the plate in front of him. When he stood up and moved out of the dining room, he didn't speak to her, tell her that it was all right now, that it was all over.

That's the way she saw it. Victoria was still alive, wasn't she? Shermie was still around, too, much to her anger. She really hated Shermie—who named their kid that?—and how much attention he got even when she was around him. Lorie was the baby, and everyone should have been focusing on her, damn it. She followed her father into the kitchen, a place she seldom went to, and asked him what was going on.

"I'm going to talk to your mother before I do anything drastic." Lorie asked him why he had to tell her anything. "Because she's my wife, and she deserves to know that her own daughter nearly killed two members of our family by being a selfish bitch." Her dad had never called her anything but his girl, and it hurt her that he used that name to call her. "Lorie, I'd like for you to leave this house. I don't want to see you until…I don't know when, if ever, I want to see you again. Your mother will call you sometime after she gets back."

"You can't seriously be thinking about kicking me out of my own home, Dad. Christ, I didn't get any of them killed. That sergeant or whatever he was called on the boat is the one that killed the Davies. That is nothing on me." He told her to get out. "Dad, you're thinking of this all wrong. I only wanted my sister to pay attention to me like she was that kid of hers. That's all. I only wanted my sister back."

"Jake." When the butler came into the kitchen after Dad yelled for him at the top of his lungs, she thought for sure that this was going to be the end of it. "Jake, please show Lorie out. And lock the doors behind her. I'd also appreciate it if you were to call a locksmith for me to have the locks changed on the house."

"Yes, sir." He looked at her, and she told him her dad was joking. One look at her dad, and she knew that she'd pushed him too far. "Ms. Lorie. If you'll come this way."

"Dad, you're pissing me off. Stop this right now before you do something that you'll regret." He told her that he had already done that by not asking her sooner about her involvement in the kidnapping of his only grandson and the near-death of his daughter. "I'm your daughter, too, dad. I took a big chance in telling the Davies that lie that made them take Shermie. They might have hurt me too. Did you think of that? Then what would you have done if they'd hurt me as well as killed off Victoria and the kid?"

The staff that was in the kitchen gasped. She glared at them, but they didn't leave the room like she thought they should have. Dad told her to get out, and instead of taking her to the front of the house, her own dad had her shoved out the back door, and it locked behind her. This was insane.

Since the car had left her there to be gassed up and washed, she didn't know that they did that to the cars, she didn't have a ride into town. She had always assumed that they stayed clean because of who they were. Silly, she realized now, but she made her way back to town. When she saw the Strong home on her way, she decided to stop in and see if she could find one of the younger men to take her out to dinner. That would show her dad that not everyone thought that she was selfish or a bitch.

"They're in the back garden, Ms. Dutch." Being

escorted to the side of the house, she had an inkling that the Strong family had more money than her family. As soon as she was waved at by the hunky men that were shirtless and had on swim shorts, she saw Shermie sitting alongside the pool with other kids. The little freak. He wasn't the least bit afraid of the water, just showing off.

"I didn't know you were coming over, Lorie. Your sister and mother are on that cruise they talked about." She smiled at the man talking to her, having no idea who he was, when he invited her to have a sandwich with them. "We've been having fun with the pool until we go into town later and have dinner."

"I'd love to go to dinner with you." He looked around and then back at her. "You did invite me, right? I mean, it would be very rude of you to tell me about dinner plans and not invite me to come along. Is my nephew and dad going?"

"Yes, to both." The man leaned back in the lounge chair. "And no, I didn't invite you. I wasn't planning on it either. I'm not into dating children."

"I'm an adult, too." He asked her how old she was. "Eighteen. I just graduated from high school last month. I'm thinking of heading out into the corporate world soon. What about you? When did you graduate?"

"A decade ago from high school and about half that from college. I'm also married with a child." She said that she didn't know. "Why should you? We don't usually hang out with you. By the way, you should know that your father called me and told me what you did to your sister. I haven't told anyone else yet, but you can be assured that I will sooner rather than later."

"You're not nice at all, are you?" He didn't answer her, and she looked around at the other men that were sitting around the pool. "Well, I guess I'm not going to be invited by any of you, but Dad will bring me along. I am his little girl."

"Whatever gets you thinking you'll be coming with us, you go on thinking that." She was tuned out then. No one would speak to her as she sat there trying to get them to notice her. Even the married man, why he thought that would matter to her if she wanted him, didn't speak to her again. Lorie watched Shermie as he splashed and played at the side of the pool, not speaking to her either.

Getting up when her dad showed up and asked her what she was doing there seemed to make them all wary of her. What did they think she was going to do, run her dad down? So when they all sat back down after her dad did, she decided to leave. But not before she did something that needed to be done.

Pushing Shermie into the water gave her such a thrill. Especially when he started screaming. Running away when the men started cursing at her, she laughed all the way to the road. She could still hear Shermie screaming, and it made her so happy that she did what she did. The little fucker was getting just what he deserved. She couldn't wait to tell her mom and sister if she ever spoke to them again that he wasn't as precious as they believed him to be. The little shit was finally getting what he deserved by keeping all the attention to himself.

Lorie made her way to the house. Just as she was getting ready to climb into the limo to be taken to the mall in Columbus, she was told that she wasn't to use the cars. Her father was taking this just a little too far. How did he expect her to have fun if he was taking things from her? Lorie decided that she was going to take a room at the local bed and breakfast and have a good time. They could all fuck off as far as she was concerned.

~*~

Toria was having such a wonderful time that she

never wanted to go home. Of course, she would. She missed her dad and son. Even her sister a little. But the sunshine and the company more than made up for— She stopped dead in her tracks on her way to the church she was going to visit when she saw Barton.

When he saw her, he smiled and made his way to her. That was when she saw Shermie. Barton pointed her out to him and he lost no time in closing the distance between them for a huge hug. Hugging and kissing her little boy was like icing on the cake for her day. But when she looked up at Barton, she knew that something had happened.

"It can wait until we have lunch if it's all right with you. Shermie told me that he's starving. I don't know how you keep up with him and food. He's going to be as big as I am." He was tense. While she didn't know why yet, she was willing to go to have a meal with them. Barton filled her in on the things that they'd seen while looking for her. "There are the most beautiful churches around here. I heard that was where we might find you."

"Just tell me if my dad is all right." He pointed to his left, and she saw her dad hugging her mom. "All right. It was Lorie then. Is she all right?"

The whispered question had him nodding and then shaking his head. When Barton changed the subject quickly, she went along with him. As soon as they were seated, Shermie hugged Barton before turning to her. He looked so upset that she wanted to leave and slay whatever dragon had bothered him. But it was Barton who started speaking about why they were there.

"We didn't tell anyone but my mom that we were coming. No one wanted you to find out through the grapevine. Your sister Lorie has been arrested." She nodded at Barton, knowing that it had to be more than that to bring them to where they were. "Lorie has been arrested for her part in the kidnapping of Shermie as well as your attempted murder."

"No." He didn't nod or make a sound as the wait staff came to the table quickly. She stared at Barton as he ordered for them. Since he was speaking Spanish to order, she had no idea what he told the woman, which had her hurrying away only to return with a bottle of wine and two glasses. There was also a glass of milk for Shermie. "I'm assuming that since you're talking about this with my son here, that he knows about it, too."

"She tried to kill me again." Picking up the

glass of wine that Barton poured for her, she drank it straight down. "Mom, don't do that. I'm fine. Scared—grandda said that I should say it the way I did when I got out of the pool that she threw me in. I was scared shitless."

Toria hugged Shermie to her and kissed him on the head. Not letting him go, she looked at Barton. She asked him to tell her what had happened. All of it. After asking her if they could order first, he said that he'd hold nothing back but to tell her every detail that he knew.

Toria didn't feel stressed about Barton doing this his way. She didn't feel upset but found herself being happy not just that her son had been with Barton again but also that he had handled it the way that he had. While she didn't know what he did, since Shermie looked fine, he'd handled it very well. It still hurt her head to think that Lorie had done this to her. She wanted details to make sure that it wasn't a mistake. Pouring her a second glass of wine, she sipped it this time.

"Lorie showed up at your parents' home yesterday morning." He told her about the conversation that her dad had had with Lorie as well as what transpired between them about the locks being changed. "While she is in jail, the locks were still changed. I think your dad was hurt very badly about what Lorie told him. I'm sure that you are as well."

"I don't know what I feel." When he took her hand into his much larger one, Toria didn't object or pull away. Feeling safe and secure in that moment, she asked him to go on. "I'm all right with you giving me the highlights right now. I don't know that I can take the entire story and get it through my head."

"She showed up at my family home. We were sitting around the pool when she sat down by Jenson and asked him out. I'm sure she meant more than that, but he, as you know, is married, and their baby was there with him." Then Barton got to the part about Shermie. "None of us expected her to shove Shermie in the pool. Luckily, I was in front of him in the water, talking to him about the upcoming trip I was taking for the family. I didn't catch him, I'm so sorry to say, but I grabbed him before he went under the second time. To be honest with you, I don't know which one of us was more afraid, Shermie or me."

Squeezing her boy to her, she held tightly onto Barton's hand while he told her what had happened about her being arrested. About how she had tried to steal a car as her dad had taken her limo privileges away from her as well as he'd stopped her credit card from being used.

"I love the idea that your father didn't have her on his accounts but had opened her a line of credit in the event that she went over budget. Whoever his attorney was telling him to do that is brilliant." Toria told him that her dad had heard other parents had had that issue when the kids had lost their card. "Whatever the reason, I'm going to keep that in mind when I have someone ask me about setting up credit for their kid."

"You're stalling. While I appreciate it right now, you can give me more information again." He nodded, then told her how her dad had been at the station house to press charges against her about the Davies. "She really did that? Told them that I was taking Shermie to London to live? Why? Because I was caring for him over her?"

"That's it exactly. She didn't care for the attention that you weren't paying her. Not only that, but she didn't like the fact that your parents weren't at her beck and call either." Shermie asked if he could go to the bathroom, but she didn't want to let him go. It was Barton who nodded at him. "But you remember the rules, right? Scream your bloody head off if anyone tries anything with you."

When he was gone, she looked at the man in front of her. Toria thought it was the first time that she'd looked at him in any other way than a man who was pushy and bossy. Looking down at their linked hands, she was happy when he asked her what she was thinking.

"Don't hate me because of what I say. Or, for that matter, judge me." He turned to look at her instead of the bathroom door. "I've fallen in love with you through my son. The way that he talks about you. And your family, but you mostly. You're nothing like I thought you were. And don't ask, please, I'm embarrassed enough right now." He lifted her hand to his mouth and kissed the back of it. "That's so nice. Is it your way of letting me down easily?" Laughing a little, she felt her eyes fill with tears.

"I love you too, Toria." The bathroom door opened, and there he stood. Looking him over, she noticed something about her son that she'd never seen before. Not, at least in the six years of his life.

His knee was bandaged. The blue and yellow sticky thing looked like some sort of hero in a cape. She put her hand over her mouth to hide the laughter when she noticed too that he was tanned like he'd been spending most of his days — without her — in the sun. There were scrapes on his elbows and his other knee. The tennis shoes that he had on, a pair she'd never seen before, were raggedy and dirty. The socks he had on might have been white at one time, but they weren't today. They, too, were dirty and not pulled up to his knees as she might well have had him do.

"Is there something wrong, Mom?" She shook her head and smiled at him. "You look like you're crying. Did I do something wrong?"

"No. Not at all. You look wonderful. Like you've been enjoying life. And doing it with gusto. What did you do to your elbow?" He told her. "Did grandda buy you a bike to learn on? I've been thinking about getting you one."

"No. Grandda Barkley had two in the barn that were my uncles. He said that there wasn't anything wrong with them, so I could use them until I wanted something bigger. We had to combine the two of them so that I'd have a working bike, but it's been fun riding it all over town and back to the house. Barton even has me go into town and pick up our lunch now that I have a big old crate on the front of it." He let her look over his hand for about ten seconds before he pulled it back. "I cried a little when I fell off the bike the first time. It was all right, though, because I was learning a new thing. But when I got hit by the tractor that was in the street, I didn't cry one bit. I'm getting braver."

"You were hit by a tractor?" Barton laughed as he explained. "Oh. Well, will you be careful about watching the stop signs from now on? That could have been serious."

"I told you she'd fuss at me." Barton asked Shermie if he'd washed his hands while in the bathroom. "Yes. This is grime that I got from working with the sander with you."

While they spoke, she watched the two of them with their heads together, talking about the sander. Apparently, Sherm, as Barton called him now, was working on the house with him daily, and sanding down the outside steps was a major project. Toria found that she didn't care. Not about him getting scrapped up. Not how dirty his shoes were nor the fact that he should have had sunscreen on while playing in the yard. He was having fun just being a kid. And that, she realized after a few minutes, was exactly what she had wanted and never achieved for him all along. To be a normal kid.

"Are you guys dating or something?" She wasn't able to pull away from Barton's hand quickly enough to — well, she wasn't sure why she wanted to pull her hand out of Barton's, but he held onto her. "That is really cool. I'm so happy for you both."

When their food was brought to them, she was too flustered. Barton helped Sherm not only with his tiny bowl of catsup, his favorite food group, but she watched his hands as he made short work of putting his napkin on his lap, too. Then they both stared at her. Shaking her head, she decided that she was going to continue to be embarrassed if she didn't get her head on straight.

"We're not dating, though I do think that we both want to, correct?" Barton said that it was something that he wanted to do very badly. "Good. We're on the same page with that. However, I don't think that he's ready for you to call him dad yet. I don't know that — what?"

"When I was pushed in the pool, I called him dad. Screamed for him as my dad." Barton told her again how he'd been in the pool when Sherm had been pushed, and he was all right with it if she was. "I'm ready for it. He's my hero next to my grandda.

Both of them. Mom, you should have seen them when I was calming down after what Lorie did to me. They were spitting mad at her, and I thought they were going to have her arrested."

They talked off and on about Lorie and the things that she'd done. Barton explained that Lorie was blaming her—of course, for her being in jail. That didn't make any sense even after he explained to her that he didn't think she was right in the head about it.

"She was sure mad at me the day she got arrested." Toria asked Barton if he'd been with her when she had been. "Yes. Your dad asked me to go to the bed and breakfast that she'd caused a bit of trouble at because her credit card no longer worked. I went there so your dad didn't have to and explained that she wasn't able to use it because of her involvement in the attempted murder of you and Sherm here." He took a bite of his croissant before continuing. "That's really good. When she told me to pay for her a room, I told her no, and she slapped me. She said that no one tells her no more than one time. That's messed up if you ask me. But she was arrested for assault then, the charges from her unknown until then involvement of the kidnapping and murder of the Davies were brought against her. She's going to be facing some serious jail time when this goes to trial."

It didn't bother her that her sister was in trouble with the law. Nor did she think she'd lose any sleep over the fact that she'd be spending a long time behind bars. Her son, who she had only just found out, would be safer, as well as the rest of her family. Which she thought would include Barton and his family as well. Smiling, she reached for Barton's hand and held it as they walked into the bright sunshine. It was going to be a better day than she could have ever imagined.

Chapter 6

Barton was glad to be home. But then again, he wasn't. He'd been to Europe before, even on a cruise ship. But this time, it had been special because he'd spent it with two people that he adored more than — he was in love. Putting another load of laundry in the washer, he set it to wash and finished folding the towels that he'd taken out of the drier in order to put his and Sherm's clothing in it.

"How come we have dirty towels, and we've been gone for over a week?" He looked at Sherm when he said he didn't know. "Okay, a better question would be, I guess is, how come there are towels here when I asked you, specially if you had brought them down before we left?"

"I forgot to bring them down." Barton pointed out that he did know then. "I guess. I did put them in the hamper, and I was planning on bringing it down, but I was too excited to remember. Being with Mom pushed all thoughts of dirty towels out of my head." When he grinned at him, Barton asked if he'd been practicing what to say about that. "Yes. Was it a good one? I'm going to use it on Mom sometime. About excitement, not about seeing her."

"She'll see right through you." He said that he'd figured that, too. "By the way, I'm going to start seeing your mom. Is that all right with you?"

"You see her all the time, Barton. I think a better way to put that—borrowing what you said was, you're going to marry my mom and live happily ever after with me as your son." They both laughed. "I was hoping that you guys would start dating. Or whatever you old people call it."

He chased Sherm all through the house just to catch him and tickle him. Barton did love this kid and thought that if he never had any other children, he'd be just as right as rain to have this guy.

"I've been thinking that I need to hire some staff after the house is finished up. They're saying that it will be at least another month before we can have the house to ourselves again. Just having it cleaned has made such a difference. He asked if he'd asked his mom if she wanted to move in. "No. I mean, she's welcome to, but I didn't want to rush things with her. I do love her. You understand that, don't you?"

"Yes. And she's happy too. I don't think she's been happy for a long time. Do you?" He said that he didn't know her before all that much, so he couldn't make that call. "Can I tell you some things about her that you might need to know?"

They were in the kitchen now of his apartment, hating it because it seemed so small now that he had his own home. They were having subs for dinner that they were going to make on their own. Thinking about the question, he decided that he did want to know some things but not personal things. And told him that.

"I want to get to know her on my own, I guess. But it would be good if you told me things that she can't stand so that I don't mistake using them. And what sort of foods does she love. And flowers. Does she like them or plants? I guess a few little tidbits would be helpful. But nothing very personal." Sherm nodded and the two of them started on their meal. "Does she have any allergies that you know of?"

"Yeah, she's allergic to liars. I didn't understand that before. I still don't know why she'd say it like

that, but she can't stand when people lie to her."
Barton said that he wouldn't lie to her. "Good. Also,
she has this weird allergy to raw carrots. It gives her
the poops. She can eat them cooked all right but not
raw."

"That is strange. But I'll remember that." The
two of them finished their meal and ate in the kitchen.
He told Sherm that he was going to donate all the
stuff in his apartment when they were ready to move
in. "Also, there is another estate auction tomorrow.
Would you like to go with me? The house has a lot of
furniture to sell off, and I thought you could find you
something to put in your bedroom."

"That's great. I wanted bunk beds. But I don't
think that I do now. I don't know anyone my age
that would...let's face it, I'm not a normal kid. I'm
going to college when I turn eight, and I'll still have
to live with my mommy. I don't think college-aged
kids would want to bunk in my room with me."
Barton couldn't help it. He laughed. "Also, you have
to admit that I'm a nerd too."

"I love you, Sherm. You are forever someone
odd, as you said, but you're the most down-to-earth
kid I've ever met." Sherm asked if he could ask
something of him. "Of course. Anytime. However,

like I told you before. Be careful what you ask because I'm not going to lie to you either."

"Good. Can I call you Dad?" Barton had to sit down. It was that, or he was going to fall on his ass. "I know that I've called you that before. And I meant it then as much as I do now. But I love you too. I've never had a dad that I know, and you've been the best that a person could ask for. Even your brothers have become my uncles. I love you—"

"I'd be honored if you were to call me dad. It... well, kid, I've thought of you as my son for so long now that I've kinda gotten used to being your father figure. So, your wanting to call me Dad will be the greatest gift that anyone has ever given me. And it's a title that I'll cherish for the rest of my life."

They hugged again, and then Barton held Sherm to his chest for a few minutes longer because he was emotional to the point of tears. After telling him that he loved him dearly, the two of them sat down on the couch in the living room when, all of a sudden, Sherm jumped up and said he'd be back.

When he came into the room again, he handed him one of the three boxes that had come in the ornaments from their last auction. He asked him what it was.

"I don't know what you have. Both my grandda's—hey. They're really going to be both my grandda's—when I gave them theirs, they were both different. So I haven't any idea what you're going to get. I hope it's not a dud. But I've been planning to give it to you since I found them. Go ahead, open it up." Opening the box, he could only stare at what was in the box. "Oh wow, yours is really different. Grandda, your dad got two ornaments like the ones in the box. He loved them. My other grandda got money. It was ten brand new one hundred dollar bills. But he thinks that since they're so old, they might be worth more, but he said that he'd never use them. But save them for when I had kids. I think he's going to be waiting a long time with that. But I think that what you got is the best."

He did as well. Pulling out the necklace that was nestled in the prettiest blue velvet was simple yet the most elegant thing he'd ever seen. There were earrings and a bracelet that was there as well. The ring, with a Tiffany-style setting of the most beautiful yellow diamond he'd ever seen, was something that he'd never seen the likes of before.

"This is beautiful, Sherm. I'm thinking that it would be beautiful on your mom. Don't you think?"

He said that he could ask his mom to marry him with the big diamond ring. "I think that I will too. Sherm, this will be something that we'll treasure for generations. We'll pass it along to you, as our oldest, and you can use it to give to your future wife. And so on down the line. I can almost see this draped around her neck. If she will marry me."

"I think that if you don't ask her, she'll ask you. Then you'll look dumb because you don't get to ask her with…you know what? I'm going to tell her to ask you to marry her. That way, I can make fun of you for the rest of your life. I guess that won't be too long, really. You're kind of old now." Tickling him again, Barton only stopped when his cell phone rang. It was his dad. "Is everything all right?"

"I just got off the phone with the police. Lorie is wanting to see her sister, but since she won't be home until the day after tomorrow, she said that she would, and I am using her words here, she would allow you to come to see her in her place. She thinks that you can talk some sense into her parents in coming to get her out of jail. I've spoken to Warren, and while he's not going down there, he asked me to call you and see if you can go. Can you?" Barton told his dad that he'd go and see her, but he wasn't going to be nice. "That's what Warren is hoping for. For you to go there and set her straight on some things. Are you going to bring Sherm here before you go? If so, he's working on a list of things that he wants to be brought up and make sure she understands. Son, it's a long list so far."

"I'll leave my place now and see you guys when I get there. Sherm and I have eaten, so you don't have to feed him." Sherm had been staying with him since they'd come back from seeing his mom and grandma. "Dad, I wanted you to be the first to know that Toria and I are going to start seeing each other when she gets back."

"Thank goodness. I couldn't love her any more than if she was my own daughter." Dad laughed. "All right, son. I'll see you soon. I don't have to remind you that they record all conversations at the jail and also to not let her drag you into whatever drama that she has. She's a rotten person, and I'm just glad that her family is going this route with what she's done to that poor boy and his mother."

As soon as they were ready to go, Sherm got into the truck with him. It occurred to him that he was going to have to get himself something bigger. Sherm wasn't big enough to sit in the front seat, and his truck only held two people. Thinking about what kind of car he would need, he nearly missed what Sherm said to him.

"I don't know what her plans are concerning your family. I should ask her but I don't know that we'll ever know too why she did what she did." Barton asked him if he wanted him to ask her anyway, and he said no. "Is there anything you want me to ask her? I will, but I doubt you'll like her answers."

"Yes. Can you ask her why she hates me so much?" Barton glanced at Sherm before pulling into his parent's driveway. "Nah, don't ask her that. Like you said, I am not going to like the answer. Do you think that she was just jealous of me? Or something like that? It seems so stupid to be jealous of a little baby, don't you think?"

"I have heard worse stories as to why people hate someone. Petty things that would blow your mind." Sherm was quiet as they went into the house. Dad gave them both a big hug and handed him an envelope. "Can I read this over now? I want to make sure that I get what Warren wants me to say."

"Yes, of course. Good idea." Warren came out of the kitchen with a cup of something hot, the steam was rolling off the top of it and a plate with a glass of milk and cookies on it. Dad explained to Warren what was going on. "This way, he can get what you need from her."

They went over the things on the list, and he was impressed at how much thought had gone into the things that he had to say. Mostly, it was a list of things that he wasn't going to do for his daughter from now on and a list of things that he was doing. He especially liked the statement that she'd no longer be welcome at his home and that he was no longer footing the bills that she had now that he'd disowned her.

"You should call your attorney soon, Warren. I'm not saying that you're going to fall over dead anytime in the foreseeable future, but you need to get yours and your wife's wills in order. Even if you only change that you're going to not leave her anything. You need to get that done as soon as possible." He said that he had an appointment with the attorney in the morning. "Good. That's the sort of thing that you don't want to wait until the last minute to fix."

After leaving the house, he made his way to the jail. He'd never been in this place but to talk to a client or something along those lines, but he looked around today. There seemed to be a great many more people there now than at any other time that he'd been there. He wondered how much it had to do with the woman/child he was going to talk to. Captain Jameson stopped him before he was escorted back.

"Two things you should know before going back. The Davies, two brothers, and a sister of the deceased family have gotten wind of what Lorie has confessed to and right now gathering themselves up an attorney to sue her. They'll have a case, too, for her being directly responsible for their deaths. Also, I can't seem to get an attorney for her. They said that it was a lost cause, so they're not even taking it on as a pro-bono case at this point. The judge will need to assign her one." He asked if there was anything else. "Yes. She's pissed off she's here. She tells everyone that goes back there that this isn't going to set well with her parents and that we should just get our heads out of our asses and let her go. She also wants to talk to her sister, which is my understanding, is out of the country right now."

"She's on a cruise with my mom and family. Warren said that they're aware of it going on here, but they're not going to leave their ship early because she's not worth it." He also told the captain that he was going to be seeing Toria, and he congratulated him on that. "I'm as happy as I've ever been, so I'm hoping that it works out for us both."

"It will. You're a great guy. If anyone tells her differently, you send her my way. I'll give her the heads up on what kind of man you are. All you Strong men are good to have in your corners." He thanked him, slightly embarrassed about being complimented. "Like I said, a good man. All righty, then. I'll get you back there so you can go home."

On the way back, he heard other inmates complaining about Lorie. How she needed to have her mouth shut permanently. It made him smile thinking that hardened criminals were complaining about one of their kind.

"Hello, Lorie. I was just thinking how much of a pain in the ass you have to be to be complained about the people that are just like you. I don't know that they're all being convicted of murder, but you're not making any friends around here." She told him that she didn't need friends unless they were all well-hung like he appeared to be. "You'll never know. What do you want? I'm Barton Strong. Tell me what has me here so I can go back home and enjoy my evening."

"I want you to find my parents and make them

come down here and bail me out. They've made their point that they're mad at me, so I've learned my lesson. Tell them, and I want out of here." He told her that he had a list of things that he was to tell her. "So? Get on with it, then. And then you have to get me out of here. This is no place for a person like me should be. I didn't do anything but tell a little lie. I can't help if they took it too far."

~*~

Toria was thrilled that Barton was there for her as she read over the transcript of him talking to Lorie. The things that she said about her and their relationship broke her heart. She really did profess to hating her. Simply because she didn't devote all her time to her whenever she wanted her to. Which, it looked to her like it was every minute of every day.

"She really is upset that I went to my husband's funeral in her birthday month? It wasn't even close to her birthday. And I believe, even though I was grieving, I did get her something nice for it." Barton asked her about her birthday being a whole month. "Yeah, you'd think she might have grown out of that, but it's now six weeks long. And she expects everyone to give her a present every day of the six weeks too. She has a register at every store online of what she wants that you can pick from, too. High-end things like worth thousands of dollars."

"What happens if you don't...never mind. I've seen her in action. And I'm going to tell you the same thing I told your dad, she's not spoiled. Not like I thought she'd be. She's off her rocker." Toria laughed, and it made her feel better. But looking at the things that she said, that she was accusing her of, just didn't make any sense. She asked Barton about one of the things on her complaint list. "I was hoping you could clear that up for me. She wouldn't tell me why she thought that her parents should have let her live on her own when she was sixteen. Lorie just said that was what they should have done. Not that she asked for it—and I'm sure your parents would have turned her down, just that they should have known to set her up in her own place, with slaves—she actually called them that, to wait on her and care for her."

"She wouldn't even get her driver's license when she was old enough because she didn't think it was right that she had to drive herself around after that. Like being carted around was something that just should have been done for her all her life." He laughed, asking her if she had ever gotten them.

"No. And that was another fight she and I had. I wouldn't allow her to use my car for someone else to drive when she was fifteen. She just wanted to use it long enough to drive to Florida to see a concert with a bunch of her friends. When she saw how it would only hold five people, she got super mad at me when I wouldn't trade in my car for a school bus for this other person to drive. I guess I knew that she was odd; I just never took it all into account before. Like the little things were all right but once I can see them all together, then I notice it. What happened to her?"

"I don't know. But she isn't understanding or doesn't want to understand why she's in trouble with the courts because she told a lie. That's all she can focus on. She fibbed to the Davies, they tried to kill you and Sherm, got killed themselves, and she doesn't understand why that's all her fault." Toria said because she lied to them and frightened them into thinking she was taking Sherm away. "Yes, well, she said it was a little bit of fun for her, not serious. Lorie then told me that people shouldn't take her all that seriously. She was only a kid back then. I don't know that she's ever been just a kid. From some of the things that your dad told me, she's always been a handful."

Toria didn't want to have to deal with anything to do with her sister. Not today nor any other time, as a matter of fact. She wanted to get her life on track and enjoy getting to know Barton. When she told him that, he pulled her up from the seat that she was sitting in and pulled her tightly to his body.

"There is nothing I'd rather be doing than getting to know you better, too. Not just you but this lovely body of yours as well." When he lowered his head to hers, she watched his eyes. As they slowly closed, so did his mouth over hers. Moaning slightly, she leaned into the kiss and showed him just how much she wanted to get to know him as well.

Christ, the man could kiss. Even as his tongue slid along her closed lips, she allowed him entrance and nearly swooned. It wasn't a word she'd ever used before, but she found that it was the perfect one to say just how he made her feel. As he wrapped his arms around her, pulling her even tighter, she had a thought that making love with this man would be just as consuming and epic as his kiss. Toria wondered if she would survive him. Or his lovemaking. When he lifted his head, all she wanted to do was to pull him back and have him continue what he'd been doing before.

"Sherm is coming." She could hear him then. Shouting from the kitchen that he'd found something. While Barton didn't completely pull back from her, he did position his body so that he was slightly behind her. It was then that he took her hand and put it on his cock. It was thick and long. Hard as stone, she knew that he was, in a way, telling her he was hiding behind her. "Don't move."

Giggling, she was ready — somewhat — to face her son when he came sliding into the room with them. Leaning down to help him up from the new flooring, Sherm managed to shove something in her face as he kicked her shins, trying to stand on his own. Finally, Barton stepped in. Pulling Sherm from between her feet and setting him on his own. It was like a comedy of errors before she realized what she had in her hands.

"Oh, Shermie. Where did you find her?" The little kitten looked fuzzy and plump. It was then that she noticed the larger cat of the same coloring standing in the doorway of the kitchen, watching them. "Is this your little one, Momma? She's a beautiful kitten. I suppose you want to take her back."

After putting the kitten on the floor in front of the mother, she nudged the baby until it was right at

Sherm's feet. He sat down beside them both, and the mother kitten climbed up into Sherm's lap like she'd done it all the time. Her son pulled the tiny kitten onto his lap, too.

"She brought her to me just a bit ago. I've been helping her out, trying to make her like me. And she does. A lot. I helped her make her a bed when Grandpa Barkley told me that she was a barn cat and meaner than a snake. She loves me." Toria said she could see that and joined Barton on the floor, too. The mother cat smelled her hand when she put it out to pet her and then looked at Sherm. "She's my mom. She won't hurt you either, I promise."

It was then that the most incredible thing happened, the mother cat laid her head on her outstretched hand as if all she needed to approve of her petting her was Sherm's permission. Even the newborn kitten seemed to approve of her after that.

"Were there any more kittens, Sherm?" He said that she had about six of them, not counting the one here. "She might need to get back to them. If they go too long alone, they might get hurt."

"I covered them up for her. She made sure that none of them moved either. She's a good momma, Dad. Grandpa Barkley said that we'll need to take us one of her babies home with us for the barn. After a while, he said we'd have more than enough to keep out the mice. Did you know that this momma cat is the grandbaby of the one that Uncle Jenson had? Grandpa told me that we'd need a good mouser, and this one might be the best." Barton told Sherm that his dad would know as he'd been watching over the cats in the barn for years at his home. "He said that he gives kittens away when they're born to people who need them. I think that's sad, too."

"The mothers can have a lot of kittens in their lifetime. To be honest, they more than likely couldn't tell you how many litters they've had if they could speak to you." Sherm thought that was even sadder. "I'm sorry. But it's the truth. That's one of the reasons that they ask people to get their cats and dogs fixed. So they won't overrun us humans."

Sherm headed out to the barn again, taking with him a can of tuna that she'd planned on making tuna salad with for their lunch. She wouldn't buy it again unless it was for the cats, however. She found out that neither Barton nor Sherm liked tuna salad. If she was honest, she didn't overly care for it either.

They made their way over to the new house around two. She kept thinking about Lorie and what she'd nearly done to the family. It was no wonder that her dad and mom were so upset with her. She was, as well. To think that anything good would have come out of the lie she told was crazy. Toria had an appointment to see Lorie after she left the attorney's office this afternoon. Her dad had removed all mention of Lorie from his will, and Mom was doing the same but to say that they weren't leaving her anything.

Like Barton did with his money and credit, she was having all her financial records changed to include both her and Barton's name. They were going to get married at the courthouse tomorrow afternoon, and she couldn't wait. Things were moving along nicely, she thought to herself.

Toria looked at the ring he'd given her last night. It was the most beautiful thing she'd ever seen. The other pieces to the set were going to be on her when she and he married, too. To start a tradition like she'd never had before. Even her parents were jealous of such a gift, and she was happy to do this for the future generations of Strong brides.

"Do you think we're moving too fast?" Toria didn't know where that question had come from. The three of them, including Sherm, had had this very conversation last night. "I know that we're not, but I worry what…well, I don't really care what people say about us getting married so quickly. But do you think that this is real love? That we're not going to hurt one another someday?"

"No, I don't." Barton led her along the staircase to the upper floors and pulled her into the bedroom that was being stripped down to the walls. "I love you. I love you like no one I've ever loved before. Was it quick? Yes. I agree with you on that. But it feels no less like we're in love than if we'd had fifty years of knowing each other. I know, with all my heart, that you're the one for me. The only one that I'll ever love because you're perfect."

"I love you as well. So very much." They toured the house. This was the second time in as many days since she got back from vacation, and she loved it all the more. The very fact that even though it was an older home, it had been well cared for and loved. Just as they were doing to it now that it belonged to them. Toria couldn't wait to move in and be a family there.

Chapter 7

Barton was glad that Toria had asked him to come with her at the last minute. She was nervous but handling the stress of it very well, he thought. He was going to make sure that she had a vacation like she'd recently had at least once a year. More if she needed it. He stayed seated when Lorie was brought in with cuffs and leg shackles on. She'd not had those when he was here the last time.

"What's happened to you?" Lorie said that she had to share her cell now, and the other person wasn't doing what she wanted. "You do know that you're not the boss of everyone, don't you, Lorie? I mean, you might think that people should bow down before you, but that's not going to happen. Especially as mean as you are to everyone you come across. Not that you'll ever take that into consideration when you think you're right all the time. All right. I'm here, so what is it that you wanted to see me about? Before you speak, I want you to know that I'm happy that you're here and not out causing the family anymore—"

"I didn't do anything, and you should just admit it. And that's another thing you're going to take care of. That attorney that I have, he's worthless. He's been telling me that I should just admit that it was my fault—though it's not, and not piss anyone else off by saying that it's not, so they don't throw the book at me. What kind of advice is that? I. Did. Nothing. Wrong. When are you people going to get that into your heads? It was a small lie, and it's not my—"

"I'm sick of hearing that from you as well. You lied, and it had consequences. End of story. Because of you, two people are dead, and two more were nearly killed. Your own family, Lorie. Can you just think about that for a moment? You nearly had your own sister and nephew killed because you were a jealous bitch that needed to grow the fuck up. Though at this point in your life, I doubt you will ever think that you're ever in the wrong." Lorie rolled her eyes at her and said that she was very mature for her age.

"Really? Tell me, why are you shackled down to the table like an animal? It's not because you're a grown-up who is mature enough to take the punishment that you deserve. You're a monster. And I am thrilled that you're in here where you can't—why did you push Shermie in the pool that day? That was childish as well as petty on your part. What has he done to you that has you lashing out every time he's near you? What did you hope to gain from that? I really want to know."

"He's faking being afraid of water. Just so he can have all the attention on him. Well, I showed him, didn't I? He's not the least bit important to me or anyone else. I wanted to prove it to the others there." Toria told her sister that she set him back to being afraid again. "Whatever. He's a little shit, and I'd appreciate it if you quit referring to him as my relative. For that matter, you, too. I'm finished with all of you. But you'd better be helping me out of here, Victoria, or I'm going to make sure that the next time you get shot up that you're not going to make it." Barton did something that he'd never done in his entire life. He wasn't going to regret it either.

Barton slapped Lorie hard enough to bust her lip and knock her back a bit so that she hit her head on the concrete wall behind her. Blood trickled down her chin onto her jailhouse uniform. The officer with them didn't move, didn't say a word but he did smile a little. When Barton stood up, putting his hand on Toria when she started to cry, Lorie demanded that he be arrested for assaulting her.

"You fucking cunt. I can't believe that—We're finished here. We'll not return to speak to you again. Just so you know, you've made an error in pissing off one of the most influential families around here, and I will make your life a living hell no matter where they put you for your sentencing." Helping Toria to her feet, she staggered slightly, and he half carried her out of the room. Once they were out of the room, he comforted her as best he could under the circumstances. "I have you, honey. You're going to be all right. I have you."

"Get your ass back here. I'm not finished with either of you. Victoria, come back here before you really piss me off." The door shut behind them, and so were Lorie's demands. Getting Toria out of the building was difficult. She just seemed to be limp. Picking her up in his arms, he was given clear passage out of the stationhouse and out into the parking lot beyond. While he didn't know what had happened to her, he was sure that she was never going to be hurt by her sister again if he could help it. Barton would go to prison for the rest of his life by killing her if it came to that.

"I'm all right." He didn't relinquish her until he was able to set her on the hood of his car. Even then, he didn't let her go. "I'm going to be all right. I promise you, Barton, I'm all right. I will be in a few minutes."

"Yes, you are. You will." She laid her head on his chest, and he held her. His heart broke when she started sobbing again. He wanted to go back into the jail and knock Lorie around again until she understood how pissed off he was. Perhaps he'd be able to knock some sense into her. But he wouldn't. He knew that would hurt Toria as well. "I'm sorry that I told her that we'd not be back. That's, of course, your—"

"I won't go back. I've been given a summons to appear for her trial, but other than that, I'm not going to acknowledge her in any way." She smiled at little. "My knight in shining armor. Thank you so much for…oh, Barton."

She cried more, clinging to him. He felt helpless with dealing with her being hurt. Loved her all the more in that moment for what she was going through. Pulling out his cell phone when he heard his dad's ringtone, he immediately asked him if he could call him back.

"Oh my, I can hear her. All right, son. You call me back." He started to disconnect when he heard his dad say for him to tell Toria that he loved her. "The both of you. I'll talk to you later, Barton."

"Dad said that he loves you." She nodded. Now that she was quiet for a few minutes, he wanted to talk to her. About what, he didn't have any idea, so he thought of something that had happened earlier when he'd spoken to Jenson. "I told Jenson how Dad had said that the cat that Sherm is taking is a relative of the cat he used to have. He pulled up his sleeve and reminded me that the cat had hated him from the start. Jenson had to have a tetanus shot as well as five stitches because he'd tried to pick the little one up. I'm talking, weighing less than six ounces, this cat tore into him like it was her job. I told him about how Sherm was not only picking the momma cat up and her kittens, but it seemed to understand what he was saying to it. He didn't think that was the least bit funny either."

"Sherm has wanted a pet since he was about

two years old. I didn't know if he'd be good to it, so I put it off as much as I could. Apparently, our boy is some kind of wild animal whisperer or something." She looked up at him. "She threatened to kill me again, Barton."

"I know, honey. I can't believe it either. They would have had to tell her that she was being recorded and that her transcript would be evidence if she said something incriminating. She's all kinds of stupid, isn't she?" Nodding to him, she pushed him back a little and stood up. "How are you feeling right now? I was very worried about you when I picked you up."

"It was as if my entire body drained of blood when she said that to me. She acted like, well, I'm not sure what she acted like in there, but she's not going to talk to me again like that. Nor will, as you said, I go to see her. She's fucked up on her own. And I'm finished being her scapegoat." He told her that he loved her. "And I love you. Why don't we go home and figure out if we're compatible sexually? Sherm is going to be spending the night with his grandparents, and we'll have the entire apartment to ourselves."

"I love the way that your mind works." He kissed her on the mouth, then pulled her close to him to kiss her again. Rolling his hips into her, just to let her know how much he wanted her when she sighed, he pushed away. "If we stay out here much longer, I'm going to take you right on top of the car. I'm sure that there will be a time when I want to do that, but not our first time. It needs to be special."

"No, I want hard and dirty." He laughed, sliding his hand down her ass and then to her groin under her dress. He watched her eyes darken as he slipped his hand into her panties. "What are you doing? That—oh yes, that feels good. Barton, we should…please don't stop what you're doing."

Sliding his fingers into the front of her panties and then into her pussy, she rode his finger while he fucked her gently with his body. He wanted to watch her face, see her eyes when they darkened more, but she wasn't looking at him. She'd closed her eyes tightly as he worked her pussy for them both.

"You're so wet. Think of what my cock is going to be doing to you when I get you naked beneath me, love." She groaned with him when she told him that she was close. "When we get home, I'm going to lay you on the bed and feast on your pussy. I want to taste you as you come down my throat. Lap at you until you have to beg me to stop. And I might, but not for long. I need you."

She came screaming out his name against his chest. Even as she came a second time, he had to hold onto her tightly before she knocked the two of them to the ground. She was bucking hard against his fingers. Not that he would have cared. Barton knew that he'd really embarrass himself by fucking her where they landed. Right in the police parking lot.

"I have never in all my life come like that." He grinned. It made him feel like he was very manly when she said that to him. "You're going to kill me when you use your cock the same way, aren't you? Christ, that was fantastic."

They didn't speak on the way home. He was busy concentrating on not just his speed but his driving, too. Every part of him was in overdrive, thinking about what they were going to do—what he was going to do to Toria when he got home. He hoped that no one was there—

"Change of plans." He turned the car around and headed for the highway. "If we go home, someone will notice, and that will be the end of us having any fun together. And I plan on having a great deal of fun with you. I'm finding us a nice little hotel room that we can hide away in."

150 Kathi S. Barton

"Make it closer rather than nicer. I don't care what it…I guess I do care, but don't take too long. I'm so close to coming that I could touch myself and come again." Barton nearly rearended a semi. All the blood from his head went straight to his cock. "Be careful. I don't want to end up in the hospital right now. I think it would be hard to explain why my underwear are soaking wet, and I smell like sex."

"I love you very much, but could you please refrain from talking about sex until we're safely in the hotel room?" She giggled, and it took just enough of the edge off of his blood pressure to ease his mind. He reached for her hand. "I love you, Toria. You're perfect for me in all ways."

Now that he was a bit less focused on getting to the hotel, he asked her if she was hungry. Picking up something quick and easy was perfect, and the two of them ate while he drove. He'd not realized how hungry he was until he pulled a hot fry from the bag and put it into his mouth.

"That has got to be the most delicious fry I've ever eaten. Give me a drink, please?" They teased one another all the way to the hotel on Forty. She'd brush his lap off, taking her time to tease him hard again, and he'd nibble at her neck and fondle her when he stopped at a light once they were off the highway. "You and I are going to rattle the hotel to the ground when we get there."

"If we make it there, you mean." He was never so happy to see a hotel sign as he was when he spied the one about ten yards from them. Pulling into their parking lot of A Grand Hotel, he was glad for two things. They were open, and he didn't see 'No' above the vacancy sign out front. "I'll wait here. I don't think that I can walk."

Kissing her on the mouth, he got out of the car. Reaching back in, he kissed her again when he reached for his wallet. Barton had to keep himself from dancing all the way to the counter and making a fool of himself. Damn, but he couldn't wait to get into their room. If they didn't have one, he wasn't sure what he was going to do. But he'd cross that bed problem if he came to it. Right now, he wanted only a hard surface to fuck his future wife on.

~*~

For a name like A Grand Hotel, the room was the tiniest thing she'd ever been in. The bed fit right in the middle of the far wall with only a few inches to spare on either side. There was a dresser that had an old-fashioned television — she thought it was called a tube television—sitting atop it. Then, a newer coffee pot was on top of the television set. A basket sat beside it with tea bags—off-brand, she thought, and some coffee pods. She laughed when she saw that the basket and pot were both chained to the back of the television.

The bathroom was only large enough for one person to be in it at a time. The shower stall, equally small, was bright yellow—almost neon yellow, with matching towels. There was a tiny sink so close to the commode that she was sure a person could use the pot and brush their teeth at the same time and not have to stretch out much.

All in all, she thought it was the most romantic room she'd ever seen. Even the yellow paisley bedspread had a pretty plastic rose on it that she thought was a nice touch. Sitting on the edge of the bed, she waited for Barton to come back to her as he'd gone to get ice for their waters for the evening. When he returned, making the room look much smaller by comparison, he pulled his jacket off and tossed it to the corner. There wasn't even a place to hang things if you needed to.

"I had to keep telling myself this wasn't a dream. That you were going to be waiting on me when I returned. Then I opened the door, and I didn't see you at first." She told him she didn't know how that happened as the room wasn't all that big. He looked around. "You're right. Did you want to go someplace else? I didn't. This is the tiniest room — I think my closet in the apartment is bigger than this place."

"No. This is perfect. It's the perfect place for us to have our first romantic encounter. If you don't count the parking lot." They both laughed, and he looked at her as he unbuttoned his shirt. "We don't have anything to wear tomorrow or whenever we leave, so try very hard to be gentle with our things. As much as I want to rip everything off of you, we do need to be practical." He pouted at her. "Do you want to have to call your family and have them bring us clothing? I'd rather not if it's all the same to you."

"They'd do it. No problem. But I'd never live it down. You wouldn't either, but I think you'd nip it in the bud faster than I would." She said that she would for him as well. "Thank you, love. However, I promise you that I'll try my best not to strip you down by tearing off your only clothing. How's that? Really, it's the best that I can do." Toria stood up and pulled off her dress, lying it on the floor where his shirt and jacket were.

Standing before him in her bra and panties, he growled low. She decided that it was the sexiest thing she'd ever heard. When he asked her to sit on the bed, that he had plans for her beautiful body, she did so without hesitation. He got down on his knees in front of her but unfastened his pants after removing his belt before settling himself between her legs. Christ, she nearly came when he kissed her navel.

Toria didn't have to check to see if her panties were soaked. She could feel the moisture running down her ass and pooling beneath her as laid there. When Barton grabbed the strings at the sides of her panties, she was panting. She was so needy again. When he didn't move, she sat up and looked at him. Her elbows held her up better than she'd been able to stand.

Her legs were on either side of his massive forearms as he rested his body weight on them, making her even more wet. He was smiling at her, a predatory smile that made her heart leap and her pussy spasm. While she watched, he ripped the material that was, at one time, her favorite outfit that she wore on the ship. He tore it not just from her hips but every part of her and lowered his head to her opening.

The first time his tongue touched her, she moved her hips up, trying to get him to go deeper inside of her. He spread her pussy by bringing his hands under her thighs and then curling them around her. Barton opened her legs further and then lifted her up. She couldn't move as much this way and thought that she'd come by just feeling trapped by him. And when he brought his fingers down closer to her pussy and pulled her open more, he started fucking her deep with his tongue. The world narrowed and centered on him and what he was doing to her.

A man had never gone down on her before. The few times she'd had sex with her husband, it had been quick and unsatisfying. They'd both been thinking of his tests when they made love the first time. Then, after that, it had never been all that good for either of them. It surprised her that she'd even gotten pregnant with Sherm. But she couldn't have been happier with the results of having him in her life.

Toria didn't think sex would ever be anything but spectacular with Barton. As soon as he sucked her clit into his mouth and began to work it with his tongue, he slipped his hand under her and pressed one finger into her pussy, and began pumping her as he worked her over. Riding him now, fucking his tongue by moving her hips, she grabbed a handful of his hair to hang on. Her hips moved as much as he would allow them up and down his fingers and his tongue.

Grabbing the sheet beneath her, Toria held it, hoping that when the moment came when she climaxed, she wouldn't fly off and shatter into a million pieces. When a second, then third finger entered her, filling her like she hoped his cock would, she began sobbing and moaning, begging him. Begging him to give her relief, to give her what she knew he could and only he could give her.

"Come for me, Toria. I need to have your nectar, all of it. Let me take your honey into me. Let me feel it slid from your hot pussy and down the back of my throat." Her body and mind shut down in that moment before she let her body go.

Her release was an explosion. There was no buildup of it only Barton telling her to come again and again. She felt her pussy flood his mouth and felt him lap her juices up. It made her next few climaxes, small ones, come quickly as he swallowed her juices.

And when he slipped his finger into her tiny hole at her ass, she came again, screaming out his name over and over as he took her higher and higher until she was ready to pass out from the force of them. When she started to come down off her high, he slipped away from her, and she whimpered at the loss.

His mouth covered hers, and she could feel her wetness on his mouth and was beyond happy of the delicious taste of her on his mouth. It was her, her juices that covered his mouth and lips, and she couldn't get enough of it. His face was wet, too, and she nearly came with just that. Licking at the taste, she groaned and pulled his lip into her mouth to taste more.

Barton's cock pressed at her opening, and she lifted her legs and wrapped them around him as he rocked deep into her. She came again, and as his cock began to piston into her faster than his fingers had earlier and even his tongue had. She sank her nails into his ribs and pulled him down so that her nipples rubbed his chest. When his tongue soothed her nipples after he suckled at them hard, Barton plunged into her, and she came again.

Her pussy began pulling him deeper, pulling him closer even as she felt him stiffen above her.

When the first splash of his cum sprayed inside of her, she screamed out his name again, sobbing and holding on to him. The heat of it bringing her over the edge and dropping her again. As he dropped onto her, she fell into unconsciousness, knowing that things would never be the same again. And she never wanted it to be.

They were awakened by a call from the old-fashioned phone ringing. The front desk calling the room to wake them startled them both awake. It was a good thing that one of them was thinking about being at the courthouse in the morning. Barton told her that he'd forgotten he'd asked the man to do that for them. She hadn't thought beyond making love to Barton, much less getting married today.

How could someone forget their wedding day was beyond her. However, getting out of bed was way more difficult than she thought it should have been. Every muscle in her body was so sore she could barely walk to the shower stall—even for how close the sucker was.

After washing her hair twice, she was ready to call it a day. She was exhausted again. However, getting to see Barton in all his naked glory had made her perk up a bit. He told her as he was washing his own hair that his brother had called, asking them where the hell they were.

"We're not even late. That's the kicker." He kissed her when he finished with the shower and came out of the stall just as she heard a quick knock at the door. "That will be Jenson. He owes me so he brought us something to wear other than the stuff we had on yesterday. And don't be surprised if he gives you a hard time about him having to bring us things. I told him that you made me take the hotel room."

Someone had purchased her a white sundress for her to wear. The flowers were there as well, and a pair of shoes like the ones that she'd fallen in love with on their trip. Getting ready, unable to blow dry her hair — there was no room for such luxuries as a hair dryer or remote control. Toria did the best she could. Making due, she was able to pull her hair back into a messy ponytail and was ready to go when he was.

The courthouse wasn't busy when they arrived. But for the limo out front, it looked like the building wasn't open. As she stood outside the building, waiting on Barton so he could talk to his brothers, her dad came out and put out his arm for her to take.

"This day, as far as I'm concerned, is one that will be in my mind for the rest of my days. I'm so proud of you, sweetie. And love you with all my heart." She kissed him on the cheek and then laid her head on her shoulder. "I want you to know that this wasn't my idea, but I love it all the same. Shermie is going to walk to you and your husband-to-be."

"Oh, Dad." She was an emotional wreck when Sherm came toward her with his suit on. It fit him like it had been tailored just for him. "You look so handsome, buddy. I might be marrying the wrong well-dressed man today."

"Mom, that's just gross." Laughter spilled from her mouth as she leaned down and hugged her son. "Do you have the necklace on, too? The bracelet looks really good on your wrist."

"Barton has the ring with him. I hope Jenson remembered to get it." Sherm said that he had remembered. "Then we're all set today."

"Not all the way set. I wanted to be the first to tell you that Jade set it up for me to be a Strong, too. I'm officially Barton's son. I hope that's all right with you." She nodded, and for the second time in her life, she was rendered speechless by a family member. "I'm now Sherman Strong. It sounds good, doesn't it? I hope that Dad is all right with it, too."

"He'll be thrilled beyond words." She heard someone coming toward them and straightened up. It was the other women of the family. Dressed in varying colors of the same dress that she had on. If they kept up with the surprises, she was going to be a royal mess by the time she said her 'I do's.'

The ceremony was short but so wonderful. Their families were there, and the judge had the paperwork all ready for them to sign that made Sherm their son. Barton was so emotional, too, that he had to breathe deeply for several minutes before he could tell Sherm how happy he was that he had him officially as his son.

"I want you to know that I will never treat you as anything but my biological son. Forevermore, I will never think of you as anyone but my true son." Sherm thanked him, embarrassed slightly himself. "If we have any more children, you will be treated the same as them. As I said, you are my son. End of story."

Jenson and Jade held a small reception for them at their home. It was just family; she loved saying that, but it was fun. She thought that her parents were the happiest. She couldn't help but notice them holding hands and staying close to each other. The knock at the door almost went unanswered, but she saw Barton go to it when the doorbell rang the second time.

"I'm pregnant. I'm here to notify you that you could be a father." Barton looked ready to collapse and might have had it not been for Jenson, who came up behind him. "The officer here is going to collect your DNA with a swab so that I can find out if you're the father or not."

"Tessa Brown, I'd like for you to meet Barton's wife, Toria Strong. Perhaps you can explain why you think that he's the father of your child." Jenson looked at Barton, and with a small nod, he told him about the hotel room. "All right. We'll get this taken care of right now. Jade, can you make a couple of phone calls for us?"

An hour later, not only was Barton swabbed, but his test results would be back in two hours. What a way to celebrate their marriage, she thought.

Chapter 8

Barton found Toria on the deck around the back. Sherm was with her, and they seemed to be having a serious conversation. Their heads were together as they spoke. It was then that he noticed that Sherm looked a great deal like his grandda Warren.

Barton was sure it was about him and the mess he was in, but he asked if he could join them, and they both smiled up at him. It was something that he'd come to look forward to. Having someone smile at you simply to say welcome. He loved his little family.

"I thought for sure that you two were going to murder me when she showed up. I'm so sorry about this." Sherm asked him why he was sorry. "It's a very special day, and I ruined it by having that woman show up at the house. I swear to you, it wasn't me that wanted this to happen."

"We know that, don't we, Sherm? Not to mention the fact you didn't invite her here. She just plowed her way in with untruths and lies. I don't believe her at all." Sherm nodded and asked if he wanted to sit with them. Toria smiled again at him when he took the offered chair. "We heard what you told your brother about the sex that morning. I no more blame you than I do myself. I will admit that I was upset at first. But then I remembered that I came to you with a son. Whatever happens, and I will admit that I don't believe for a moment that you're the only one that she's been sleeping with, but whatever happens, we'll go on with our lives. I don't know how yet, but we'll get there. I guess it would depend on how you want to handle it if she is carrying your child."

"I don't know. I've been thinking about it. I'll support her and the baby if it's mine. But other than that, I don't want anything to do with her." Toria thanked him for that. "Jade was able to find out how many other men she's getting results from, and it's seven people, men, I suppose."

"She's been busy, I guess." Barton laughed at Sherm's comment, then stopped, asking him if he knew what he'd just said. "I do know about sex, Dad. I might only be six, but I go to high school now, and those guys are forever talking about sex. Gross. And they're nearly having it in the hallways. Double gross."

"You think that now, kid, but in about ten years, that's all you're going to be thinking about. Sex. Sex. Sex. We'll be lucky to get you out of the bathroom. You'll be so ready for your own encounter." Sherm stood up and said that he was going inside. Maybe they'd want to talk about the weather or something, he told them as he was headed toward the door. When he left them, Barton reached out for Toria's hand, and he was so relieved when she took it. "I am sorry, honey. I know better than to have unprotected sex with a woman. My parents taught us that from the first day we noticed girls. They told us that some women, not all, would want to get with us to get to the money that the Strong family has."

"We had unprotected sex, too, you know. Really good mind-blowing sex but unprotected, too." He asked her if she was all right with that. "I find that I'm more than all right with that. I would love to have several children with you. Soon, too, if you'd not mind."

"As many and as often as you wish, love." He stood up and picked her up from the chair to sit her on his lap. While he did want her, right now wasn't the time. They all needed to know if he was going to be a father to Tessa's child. "I have some things that I more than likely should have told you a while ago. I'm wealthy. So, in turn, you are too. Neither of us would ever have to work another day in our life, and we'd have more than enough money to put a dozen children through college. It's not just money, though there is a lot of it, but we together have houses, land that we rent out as well as businesses that I've been able to invest in from the ground up. I'm careful with what I have and have invested very well."

"I kind of figured that you had a lot of it. The way you guys go about your day makes me think that you don't spend it willy-nilly, either. Just so we're clear on our kids, including Sherm, I don't want them to be rotten just because there is money around. I don't want to have...I don't want to have another person like Lorie in my life. I will nip that sucker in the bud right from the start. However, I do have a bit of money to tell you about now that we're talking. Nothing like what you're saying you have. But enough...I cashed in the insurance policy for when Sherman died and put it away for Sherm to be able to go to college. I did that because, for the life of me, I couldn't think that I'd ever be in love again. However, now that I've met you and really fallen in love, I realize that what I felt for Sherman wasn't true love. I think that we were both settling for each other. Sherman told me when he was lucid one day just before he passed that he didn't love me. Not like he thought that he should have. I didn't know at the time if he was just saying that because he was dying. Now I realize that neither of us loved like we should have." He asked her what she meant about settling. "Sherman was a year older than me. I was in kindergarten when we met, and I never dated anyone else. We married right after I graduated high school. Sherman was nineteen. It was...I wanted to get away from the house because of my sister, and he needed someone to hang on his arm. Eye candy, he told me. I still, to this day, have no idea what he meant. I didn't meet his parents until later, as I said. I sometimes wish that I had. I wouldn't have married him, I don't think, had I known them. But then, I wouldn't have had Sherm, and he's the best part of us. Sherman was smart, too. Like off the charts smart. But nothing like Sherm is."

"That's all so sad, and my heart hurts for you. You'll never think that I don't love you, I hope. I will tell you and show you daily how much you and any family that we have mean to me. And I'm glad that you had Sherm, too. He's the greatest kid." She agreed with him. "When this is over with everything—I mean the trial as well, the three of us will take a vacation. Sherm enjoyed flying, so I think we can make that work for us. Maybe we wouldn't go far, but maybe to someplace out west when the colder weather settles in here. But I do want to be here for the holidays if that's all right with you."

"I love that idea." She leaned her head on his shoulder. "Before we know it, he'll be going back to school, and then it'll be the holidays again. I bet you guys go big when it comes to Thanksgiving and Christmas."

"We do. It sort of snuck up on this last year. Jenson got married in the New Year. Then there was one thing after the other with things going on." The door opened behind him, and he turned when Toria did to see if it was his brother. "Hi, Dad. We were just talking about how time flies around here. What to join us?"

"We were going out to get some food to bring

back here. I know that you guys didn't have any plans for your honeymoon, but with this other going on, I was wondering if we could persuade you to join us here. At least until we have an answer." Toria told his dad that was a brilliant idea. "I'm not sure how I should feel about this woman. I will admit, I don't much care for her. Just coming here like she did, well, it sort of pisses me off. And the way that she's talking to your grandparents sort of makes me want to slap her. But I won't. Everyone is stressed, and I'm trying very hard to take that into consideration, too."

"I'll talk to her about how she's treating them." Dad told him that he thought that his grandma was going to take care of her. "Good. She will, too. Dad, I'm profoundly sorry that she came here and not to my place. A phone call would have been better, I think. But also, Jenson and Jade have been able to help, too, so that's good." Dad waved him off and sat down. "Mom is all right, isn't she? I hate that she was so upset earlier."

"She and Shermie are baking cookies. You know that's your mother's way of dealing with her stress. Though I have to admit, it's nice to smell the house full of sweet smells. I associate it with such good memories." Dad looked out over the backyard before turning to them with a smile. "I do hope you two are all right with what's going on. I no more believe that it's your child than I think that it might be mine. She's playing you, son. You know that, don't you?"

"I don't know what her game is, to be honest. She told me that she didn't want children. I didn't either at the time. Toria and I were just discussing that. We're going to have a dozen or so to start with them work from there." Dad laughed. He laughed hard, too, and it made him smile. "I will take responsibility for it if it turns out to be my child. But I want nothing to do with her."

"Good boy. I knew you were going to be that way." Dad stood up. "It's nearly time for the results. I was hoping that we could get some food in us before that. I miss all of you boys, and a little dinner with us will go a long way in soothing our minds, too. I'm going to go in and see how far they are about food."

When Dad went into the house, he held Toria to his chest. It was getting close to dinner time, and he felt his belly rumble a little in thinking of having dinner with this families. Both of them. Toria stood up, and he asked her if she was all right.

"I am. Very much so. I'm going to go and see

your mom and see if I can snag me a warm cookie just out of the oven. If Sherm hasn't eaten them all." She leaned over, giving him a quick kiss on the mouth. Would you do me a favor and see if we can use the house now? Sherm told me earlier that one of the construction workers said they might have the upper floors finished today. I'd love to spend the night there with you."

"Great. I'll give them a call now." She nodded and headed for the door. "Toria, I love you with all my heart."

"And I find that I'm the luckiest woman around to have someone love me as much as you do." She smiled. "Get on the house news. If we're going to stay there, we're going to have to pick up some things from your apartment that we'll need. Like extra clothing. I have a good mind to tear yours off of you now." With that, she went into the house, leaving him there with lust in his mind and his cock rock hard.

When his cell rang, it took him several seconds to figure out what the noise was. After pulling it out and answering it, he was shocked to hear from the contractor at their home. Telling him that he was just going to call him had both men laughing. He said that not only were the upper floors finished, but the house was finished.

"Your dad came by a couple of days ago and asked if we'd hire a bit more crew to get it finished up. He told me that you were getting married today, is that right?" He said they were married just a couple of hours ago. "Well, congratulations, young man. This is good news for you then. Your house is ready for you and your family. The landscaping needs a bit more work, but your mom told me that you were going to work in the gardens with her this fall. That's a wonderful project for you guys. Great memories. Anywho, you guys can move in anytime. Also, just a heads up, there are things here to make the house welcoming to the three of you — I just love that son of yours, by the way. Linens and such from your family. Food, too, is packed in the cabinets. You have a good family, Barton. I hope you tell them that all the time." Barton was touched and told the man that he was happy to have them in his corner. "All right then. Like I said, the landscaping isn't finished, but it doesn't look bad. And congratulations again on your marriage."

Going into the house to find Toria and Sherm, his brother Jenson was on the phone. Asking him to wait for a moment gave him the idea that his brother had the results. At that moment, Barton wasn't sure whether he wanted to know what they were or not. He didn't want to deliver good news, only to follow it with bad news.

When he hung up and turned to look at him, he smiled before speaking. "I had an idea to tease you about it to make you more uncomfortable, but Jade convinced me that it would be cruel to do that to you, especially on your wedding day. I had to agree with her. You're not the father, buddy." Barton nearly knocked his brother back when he grabbed him for a hug. Tears of relief fell down his cheeks as he thanked him. "I'm sorry that you had to go through this, Barton. I truly am. But I think this was a good thing for the other two to think on. Maybe even Sherm a bit too. Keep it in your pants if you can't cover that sucker up."

"You know it. Christ, I can't wait to tell my wife. My wife. Shit, Jenson, that might be the first time I've said that. I have a wife and a son." Hugging his big brother again, he told him what he'd found out about his house. "We'll be there tonight, so don't call unless you want me to come at you with something sharp."

"Sherm can stay here if he wants. I think that Mom and Dad invited him to stay with them, too. I think the pool, even though he'd not been in it, is a big draw for him. I see him getting over his fear of it sooner rather than later." Nodding, Barton hugged Jenson again. "I love you, Barton. Very much."

"I love you too. Tell Jade I appreciate her calling in a couple of favors for us." He said he'd tell her. Then he went to find Toria. Both she and Sherm were so excited, more for the house being done than the kid, but he was happy all the way around.

~*~

Sherm ended up staying with Jenson and Jade. He was glad that he loved his brothers enough to trust them. He also told him and his mom that he was ready to see someone about the fears that his aunt had instilled in him. Barton just knew there was more to it than just him being afraid of water. There was also his slight fear of being alone. But being willing to work through the fears was half the battle. Barton thought it was like admitting something that no one would ever think about you.

It took them until around midnight before the house was put together. Not everything, but enough that they could cook if they wanted and watch some television. He didn't know which one of his brothers had gotten them the TV, but he was glad for it. It made the house seem more alive than just the two of them wandering around a mostly empty home. They still had a lot of things to get yet.

The beds were made up for the three of them. Sherm had been able to score a bunkbed at the last auction, and he enjoyed having them sitting on either end of the room. The desk he'd gotten that went with it had to be cleaned, and it made it to the house with the dining room set. He and Sherm had put the China set in the cabinets when they'd been at the house the day before. He found Toria in the kitchen reading over the instructions on how to use the coffee maker.

"It says here that it doesn't recommend using one of those off-brand fillable pod things. I think that they only say that because it's more expensive. I'm making me a cup of tea. Do you want one too?" He said that he did and sat at the large island to watch her. "Lizzy said she doesn't drink coffee, but when someone uses her coffee maker to make a cup of it, she can taste it in her tea. So we'll get us another one for coffee if you want that."

"I don't drink coffee. I don't know that any of my family does, now that I think about it. The coffee that she's referring to is when Clay had a meeting with his people, and one of them brought their own coffee with them. Clay never let the man live it down that he ruined tea for his wife." They both laughed. "When we were putting things away, I noticed that there were some cookies. Want some of them? I'm not hungry, but I could use a couple of cookies to go with our tea."

They drank two cups of tea each and had some of the cookies. His mom had sent over a tin of the ones that they'd baked for Sherm, and he wasn't going to get into his stash without his permission. Sherm told him that he had a lot of making up to do with his new grandparents and he wasn't going to miss a moment of it.

Once they finished cleaning up after themselves, they headed up to bed. It was nearly midnight then, and he was exhausted. However, it was their wedding night, and he wasn't going to miss this, no matter how tired he was. As soon as they were in the bedroom, he pulled Toria into his arms and kissed her with as much passion as he had that had been building up all day.

"Take off your dress. Please? I want to see you, feel you." She nodded and told him that she wasn't wearing anything under it but panties. "Christ woman. You're the best thing that has ever happened to me. In all my life."

Her fingers shook as she worked the buttons through the holes. He wanted to move her hands and do it himself, but he was much too needy, and he was afraid of hurting her. But Christ, oh mighty, she was the most beautiful creature he'd ever seen.

"It's my wedding night, and I've never been so nervous in her life. Not even with my first marriage." She looked up at him. "I guess that's not something I should be talking about, should I? I'm sorry."

"No, love, it's wonderful that you're more nervous now. I couldn't love you anymore for it. But if you compare me to him, I'm going to go to the corner and sob a bit." She laughed, just as he had hoped. It seemed to make her less shaky, too.

When the dress was pulled down to her waist, she pulled it off her shoulders and cupped her bare breasts. His cock ached. When he moved closer to her, she opened her legs to let him in. Cupping his hands over hers, he lifted both her hands and her breasts up. Lowering his head, he took the hard nipple in his mouth and nipped at it gently. Her moan was rough and long.

"Please, Barton. I need you. I want you." He nodded, his mouth so dry he couldn't get a word past his lips. "You've been teasing me all day, and now I want results. And to come until my head explodes."

When she wove her fingers into his hair and pulled him tighter to her, he opened his mouth wider over her breast and sucked hard. She arched into him and tightened her grip on his hair. Barton moved his hands down her ribs, then over her hips to her ass. Pulling her forward, she wrapped her legs around his ribs and held him.

"Stand up, baby. I want to take your pants off and taste you. The smell of your arousal is making me wild with the need to taste you."

"No. Not this time. It's my turn. You stand up and take your pants off. I want to taste your cock when you come down my throat. I want to feel your cock in my mouth." He nearly came when she kissed him on the mouth, his body so ready for hers.

She dropped her legs from around him and pushed him back. He wasn't sure if she had lifted him up—nothing would surprise him at this point, or he just moved without realizing it. But suddenly, he was up and leaning against the desk, and she was running her fingers up his ribs and over his nipples.

When she tweaked one of them, he growled deep in his chest.

"Don't play too long, little girl. I'm a man with a powerful need to make love with you. If you keep this up, you could find yourself leaning over that chair with my cock deep inside of you. Take me, Toria. Take me in your mouth and suck me."

Barton watched as she gripped the zipper to his pants in her teeth and pulled it down. His cock moved over her cheeks as she rubbed against him. The drop of pre-cum at the tip was quickly lapped up when she ran her tongue around the blood-engorged head.

"Baby, please. You're killing me. I'm not going to be responsible for what happens if you don't take me now."

His head felt as if it blew off his shoulder a moment later when she wrapped her lips around him. Grabbing the back of her head, he held her to him as he moved in the heat of her mouth.

Toria's tongue was relentless. She swirled it around and around him until he was sure she had several tongues moving over him and not just the one. When she licked him along the heavy pulsing vein and down his length, he felt his balls tighten up until he was strangled by them. His spine tingled with the need to come. Guiding her head back up to his cock, she took him deep.

Barton didn't want to hurt her, but he couldn't seem to stop fucking her mouth hard. When Toria reached between his legs and rolled his tight sac in her palm, he came. Harder and faster, he pumped, filling her mouth and her throat with his cum. When the last wave shot from his cock, he jerked her head away and pulled her head up to his. Devouring her mouth, he moved them to the floor. Need made him not care what happened to her clothing. Her remaining clothing ripped from her body even as she wrapped herself around him.

"No. Over. Over onto your belly. I'm going to fuck you hard, Toria. And when you come, I'm going to come in you like you've never felt before. I need you. All of you right now."

Toria moved to the floor quickly. She may have said something, he wasn't sure, but the roaring in his head, the blood pounding through his body made him an animal. A beast in him rose up, and he couldn't stop wanting to fuck her hard if he tried.

When her ass was raised up before him, he grabbed her hips and slammed deep. Her pussy, hot and soaked, took him. Her answering primal cry gave him added strength. He slammed again and again, gripping her hips so tightly he knew in the back of his mind she'd wear a bruise because of him. She didn't pull away. With every surge forward, she rammed back just as hard, taking him deeper into her heat. Leaning forward, nipping hard at her shoulder, he growled in her ear when all he wanted to do was come deep inside of her.

"Come. Come now." And she did. When she screamed out his name, Barton pulled her body up so that her back was to his chest and kissed her. Tasting a bit of her blood on his tongue made him sorry for hurting her, but he wasn't going to stop. His tongue made love to her mouth as desperately as he took her body.

He took her deeper than he'd ever done with anyone during sex before, and she gave to him as much as she took from him. It was more than he could have imagined, making love to his wife for the first time.

"Come for me, baby. Come again so that I can try and plant our child within you." Her scream nearly had him pulling away, but he felt her pussy tighten around his cock to the point of nearly painfulness.

He felt his own climax take him, leaping over him like he'd been hit with a lightning bolt. It took him by surprise.

They both came a second time, not nearly as hard, but he was sure if they had, it would have surely rendered them both unconscious. As it was now, he was weak in the knees, and he felt like one misstep and he was going to end up face-planting himself on the floor.

Barton just managed to get them both to the bed. Toria frightened him a little when he realized that she was out and he couldn't wake her. But in the end, she told him not to touch her, or she wasn't going to be responsible for how much pain she put him in. Laughing, he got up to use the bathroom and then got into bed with her. Her body immediately snuggled tightly against his, and he closed his eyes.

"Barton, I love you." He told her that he loved her too. "I hope we have a baby soon. I want to be as happy as I am right now. Nothing in this world would make me love you any less than I do right now."

When he tried to speak around the lump in his throat, he realized that she'd fallen asleep. Pulling her closer to him, Barton thought of all the things he was going to do with his new family. First and foremost, he was going to make sure that they knew that he loved them. Just as his father and mother had done for them.

As he drifted off, his body nearly liquid, he was so relaxed that he remembered that he had made plans with Sherm to go to an auction. The kid was addicted to them now. Also, they needed to figure out if there was any word on the coins they'd dropped off to be appraised. Life, it seemed, just kept getting better hourly, he thought. And he'd have it no other way. Barton was in love. And loved. That was more than he ever hoped for in his life.

Before You Go...

HELP AN AUTHOR

write a review

THANK YOU!

Share your voice and help guide other readers to these wonderful books. Even if it's only a line or two, your reviews help readers discover the author's books so they can continue creating stories that you'll love. Log in to your favorite retailer and leave a review. Thank you.

AWARD WINNING, BESTSELLING AUTHOR

Kathi Barton, a winner of the Pinnacle Book Achievement Award and a best-selling author on Amazon and All Romance books, lives in Nashport, Ohio, with her husband, Paul. When not creating new worlds and romance, Kathi and her husband enjoy camping and going to auctions. She can also be seen at county fairs with her husband, an artist and potter.

Her muse, a cross between Jimmy Stewart and Hugh Jackman, brings her stories to life for her readers in a way that has them coming back time and again for more. Her favorite genre is paranormal romance, with a great deal of spice. You can visit Kathi online and drop her an email if you'd like. She loves hearing from her fans. aaronskiss@gmail.com.

Follow Kathi on her blog: http://kathisbartonauthor.blogspot.com/

www.ingramcontent.com/pod-product-compliance
Lightning Source LLC
Chambersburg PA
CBHW032009170626
46807CB00006B/2719